SNOWED IN LOVE

A HOLIDAY ROMANCE NOVEL
BOOK 4

AMANDA SIEGRIST

MERRY CHRISTMAS.

MAY YOUR DAYS AND NIGHTS BE FILLED WITH HOLIDAY CHEER!

·

1

———

BRUSHING off a light dusting of snow from his shoulders that had accumulated from the short walk from his car to the hospital, James headed for the front desk counter with a smile. An easy-going smile, the one he always used around Erin, the prettiest nurse that worked here.

Oh, man, he hoped his smile never betrayed how much he truly liked her. Because if she knew, she'd laugh in his face. He was so out of her league, it *was* laughable.

"It started snowing, huh? I was hoping the snow would wait until Christmas," Erin said as she reached out and brushed some lingering snow that he missed.

A shiver rushed down his spine, his smile faltering. Then, like a light switch, he snapped out of it and chuckled. He had to hide the fact that her small touch awakened too many yearnings he knew he couldn't control if she touched him again.

The sweet smile on her face only intensified the massive crush he had on her. He wanted to vault across the counter, pull her into his arms, and kiss her breathless. Kiss her until she whispered his name in undying pleasure and begged him to take her away.

Away from this dumb town.

Away from all his problems.

Her brows started to wrinkle with a frown, which made him realize he was staring at her like a lovesick fool.

"It's not coming down too bad." He shrugged, hoping it would help shake off the nervousness he experienced any time he talked to her. Then he took off his hat and ran a hand through his hair. "But if it keeps it up, we'll get a huge dumping of snow. Christmas isn't too far away. Only four days."

Something he hated to think about. Christmas wasn't a joyous time of year for him.

"Well, I didn't want the snow just yet." Her smile deepened. "I do love how pretty it looks, though." Her brows pleated. "What are you doing here so early? You usually don't start until ten."

His heart started to pound, even knowing it was ridiculous to think she knew his schedule because she secretly crushed on him—like he did with her. But he couldn't control how his heart reacted to the simple things she said. In all likelihood, she knew his schedule because it was a small town. He wouldn't be surprised if the entire town knew his damn schedule. They knew everything else about his messed up life.

Judgmental busybodies. Every single person.

Nobody knew how to stay out of your business.

That was one reason he wanted to ditch this town and run away from it all.

Except he couldn't.

He couldn't leave his sister, Theresa. Some days, she was the only one keeping him on the straight and narrow. The only one keeping him strong and resisting the temptation to have a drink.

Well, her and his sponsor, Terry. He couldn't leave either one of them.

Refusing to let any wallowing pity touch him, at least when talking to Erin, he smiled. "Dr. Pearson wanted to see me. He called and asked me to come in early." His lips twisted into a sardonic gesture. "I'm surprised the whole damn hospital doesn't know already."

Sweet laughter, like the first taste of a delicious bowl of chocolate ice cream, floated his way. "It's the first I heard about it. Maybe you're getting a raise. You've been here for almost a year. It's about time."

He didn't want to hurt her feelings, it was the last thing he would ever do. The smile on his face stayed firm, even though he suddenly wanted to punch something. Or find a drink. A delicious, strong drink would be nice.

"Not quite a year. I still have three more months until my anniversary. Who knows why he wants to see me." James tapped the counter, the urge to flee strong. "I better go. Drive safe when you leave."

"Of course. Always."

He turned around and headed toward the hallway that would lead him to Dr. Pearson's office, the head doctor of the hospital. His wife was the administrator. They married two years ago in the summer. That had been a dark time for him, trying to stay away from alcohol, getting his life back on track. He didn't know Dr. Pearson and his wife that well, not like some of the other townsfolk, but they were easy to work for.

They were the first people to give him a chance when most other people refused.

He had a record.

He once had a drinking problem.

He was now trying to straighten his life and live like an abiding citizen. One that Theresa could be proud of. He hated when he saw the disappointment in her eyes.

It also grated on his nerves that Theresa suspected he liked Erin more than he should. She was always nagging him to ask her out.

Yeah, right. Like Erin would ever say yes to him.

But it wouldn't hurt to offer her a ride home after work. His car might not look like a winner, but it ran like a newborn kitten. He made sure his car was always in working order. Erin's car, on the other hand, didn't always run so smoothly. It got stuck in the snow so much, he forgot how many times he helped her out of a jam last winter.

Yeah, he would at least offer to make sure she got out of the parking lot okay.

He almost turned the corner, then swiveled back around and decided to let Erin know he could give her a ride home. Frozen in his spot, he hesitated to make a move when he saw Marybeth at the counter.

She was just one of the many people he couldn't stand.

She didn't care what people thought about her. Or talking quietly, apparently.

"What did James want? How can you stand talking to him?"

Erin frowned. "He's very nice."

"He also has a record." Marybeth leaned forward, resting an arm on the counter. "He's bad news, Erin. I hope you're not getting any ideas."

"Any ideas?"

"Like dating him or something weird like that." Marybeth laughed haughtily. "Watch out. I swear there's something in the water around here. Someone is always getting engaged or married around Christmastime. You don't want to be next. And you certainly don't want it to be with James."

"I would never..."

He whipped around and stalked away, refusing to hear Erin finish her sentence. He knew exactly what she was going to say. She would never date him. Of course not. He knew this.

Yet, a small part of him thought maybe she might consider it. One date. Dinner somewhere nice.

Whatever. Nothing new in his shamble of a life.

Stopping outside of Dr. Pearson's office, he knocked on the doorframe, then entered when Dr. Pearson waved him in.

"Have a seat, James."

Sitting in the chair, he tried to keep still and not bounce his knee or fidget or give away how anxious he was to be called into work early. It was odd. Tension filled him up instantly when he received the call not more than an hour ago to come in two hours before his shift started.

He didn't do anything special around the hospital. Simple janitorial work. Mundane tasks, like empty the trash cans, sweep the hallway floors. He didn't venture into patients' rooms often, and when he did, they were empty. He didn't have much contact with others unless it was passing them in the hallway with a broom in his hand.

Dr. Pearson looked stern and serious. It didn't bode well. His fingers started to twitch. He could really use a drink right about now.

"Some concerning things have come to my attention." His eyes narrowed.

James nodded, unsure what he was supposed to say. He had no clue what Dr. Pearson was talking about.

"We've had some prescription drugs go missing."

He tensed.

Shit never changed.

"A few pills here and there. Nothing too obvious. At least not to where we'd notice at first."

That drink he wanted, he desperately needed it right now. It wasn't a *want* anymore. It was a damn necessity.

"After a thorough investigation, we've found the culprit."

A thorough investigation? Yeah, right. More like they found drugs missing and immediately assumed the guy with the prior record and drinking problem liked to do drugs as well. They figured *he* had to be the culprit.

Dr. Pearson frowned. "Do you have anything to say, James?"

He shrugged, knowing whatever he said wouldn't make a difference. Everyone always thought the worst of him.

Dr. Pearson averted his gaze as he rearranged a few papers on his desk. "We've decided not to press charges against you." He looked up. "You honestly have nothing to say?"

"It's snowing out. Might turn into a blizzard."

Dr. Pearson's brows burrowed into a severe frown, then he clasped his hands together on the desk and leaned forward. "I hate to have to do this, James, especially so close to Christmas, but you're fired."

Well, that was that.

James stood up and smiled a cheesy ass grin because what did he care what these people thought. "Merry Christmas, Dr. Pearson."

Then he walked out of the office with his middle finger in the air.

"I WOULD NEVER THINK James is a bad choice. He's a great guy." Erin had enough of Marybeth and her judgmental presence.

"You're wrong, Erin. He's the worst kind of guy."

Erin stood up from her chair and leaned closer to Marybeth, her eyes narrowing. "And you're the worst kind of woman. Do you ever have anything nice to say about someone?"

Marybeth jerked back, a hand to her chest. "I meant no offense. I'm only looking out for you."

Highly doubtful, but it wasn't something Erin wanted to get into with her. "Was there something I can help you with, Marybeth? I am very busy."

"No. I'm visiting Pierce. He's taking me out to lunch later and I wanted to confirm our plans."

Erin wanted to roll her eyes but settled with a small grin. "Enjoy."

Marybeth waved in her stuck-up way she always did and walked away.

Slumping in her chair, blowing out a breath, Erin finally rolled her eyes. She didn't grow up in Mulberry as Marybeth had, but she knew a good person when she saw one. Having moved to Mulberry five years ago to help her uncle with her aunt, who had early stages of Alzheimer's, it didn't take her long to fit in. Or to figure out who the gossiper was, the pest, and the person to avoid. Marybeth happened to fit into all three categories. Since she started dating a new doctor recently hired, Dr. Pierce Colton, Erin saw her a little too much for her tastes.

She didn't care what Marybeth had to say about James. Sure, she knew he had a record. Not much was kept a secret in this town. She also knew he was a recovering alcoholic. But he was trying. He was attempting to get his life back on track, staying clean for the past two years. He found a good job at the hospital as a janitor after struggling to find a place that would hire him. He was working toward a better life.

He was sweet and kind to her, stopping by her desk to say hi, or if she was on the phone, waved a quick hello. He always had a handsome smile and a warmth in his eyes she didn't see from other people, especially guys.

He might be considered one of the bad boys of the town, but she liked him. Like, really liked him. A massive crush that surprised her he hadn't caught on to yet. She swore she blushed a bright red tomato every time he stopped to chat with her.

Her last serious boyfriend, Tommy, over five years ago before she moved, hadn't been a disappointment or a bad boyfriend at all. It simply didn't work out. She wanted to move to help her uncle and he didn't want to follow.

Considering they were only twenty-two at the time, she couldn't blame him. They had been in their last year of college. She had wanted to be a nurse and he wanted to go to law school. There was no way she would've held him back from his dreams. They still talked now and again. Friendly chit-chats about how life was going.

While there were some great guys in Mulberry, only one stood out to her since the first hello ever uttered.

James Brennen. Local bad boy. But sweetheart extraordinaire.

Erin almost jumped when the phone rang on her desk. Chuckling, she couldn't believe she let her mind get so distracted that the phone scared her.

"This is Erin. How may I direct your call?"

"Erin, please make sure James Brennen leaves the hospital without incident. Call security if you have to."

Her heart started to pitter-patter like a stampede of elephants.

"Excuse me, Dr. Pearson? I don't understand."

"He does not work for this hospital anymore. He left my office and should be coming your way. I wanted to inform you he is to leave immediately."

And beware he could hurt you were the unspoken words. Erin wanted to hiss in the phone nasty, vibrant words that would probably get her fired. Why did everyone assume the worst about James? Why was he fired? What happened?

"Yes, sir. I understand."

That was the most she could get out. Her blood was boiling. Her hands were shaking. She wanted to scream and stomp her feet in support of James. First Marybeth and now Dr. Pearson.

"Call security. Just in case, please."

A tiny breath escaped before she said, "I don't think that's necessary, sir. I'm not sure why James was fired, but he would never hurt me or cause a scene. I will make sure he leaves peacefully. Don't worry about it. I do believe the patient in room ten is waiting on you, sir."

She hung up the phone before she put her job on the line. Her heart, now pounding even crazier, felt like it was about to burst out of her chest. She never spoke to Dr. Pearson that way. In fact, when she first started, he always made her so nervous with his handsome looks, his smooth words, and his kindness in how he treated his patients.

She never imagined speaking to him in such a way. Or hanging up on him.

Until now.

Until she had enough of the treatment against James. It certainly wasn't the first time she told someone to mind their business when she heard them whispering about him behind his back.

So what he had a record. So what he had a drinking problem once upon a time. It didn't make him a bad person. That's exactly what she told each and every person that dared to utter a nasty word about him.

Standing up when she saw James turn the corner, she started to come around the counter. "James? Are you—"

"You have a pleasant day, Erin. Please drive safe later." He paused in front of the automatic doors to put on his hat, getting to the exit faster than she could walk around the counter.

"Of course I will. I'm sorry—"

"So you knew I was getting fired?" His eyes turned down, his fists clenched. Then his head jerked up. "Goodbye, Erin."

He walked out before she could fix the misunderstanding. She had no idea he was going to get fired. She didn't even know why he was fired.

By the way he whispered goodbye, she'd never get the chance to speak to him again.

2

SLAMMING the bottle on the counter, he almost wished it would've shattered. Then the liquid would've splattered everywhere, preventing him from opening it and downing the entire contents in one swallow.

He wasn't a fan of Vodka, but it had been the closest thing to the register when he stalked inside the liquor store. *Get in and get out* had been the mantra in his head as he pulled into the parking lot and walked inside the store.

His hand shook as he let go of the bottle and took a step back.

Seven hundred and thirty-six days he had been sober. Days he had stayed clean and away from a bottle. Some days, it was so hard he wanted to cry, especially in the beginning. And crying didn't seem like a manly thing to do, even when his sister whispered in his ear that it was okay.

Because yeah, he had cried twice in front of his sister. Once when he apologized for the way he treated her for so many years before he finally got help. The second time had been when they got notification last year that their dad died in a car accident. He had been drinking and driving. Thankfully, he only killed himself in the process. He didn't even want to think how he would've felt knowing his dad killed somebody else, too. It was bad enough his dad was dead.

That had been another eye-opener and served as a reason he had to stay clean and sober.

Some nights, some days, he had cravings for a tiny sip of alcohol, it consumed him so badly he didn't think he'd survive. In those moments, he called Terry. His rock. His savior. The man who helped him see clearly when he couldn't. He needed a barrier between him and the bottle.

Theresa was also his rock. She said she would be there for him. She said she would help him through his pain. She did. When he called her in a funk, she came without blinking, talked to him, sometimes sat with him in silence.

He should've never stopped for the alcohol. He remained strong this long, he could keep doing it.

Yet, the bottle stared at him, mocking him. Laughing at him. Like everyone else in town was doing right now.

We knew he was bad news.

You should've never hired him in the first place.

Once trouble, always trouble.

Just a few things he heard when they didn't think he was around. Blending in was a forte he mastered. Blending into the background, sneaking into bars underage. Blending into the night when he wanted to break into his sister's house and steal her money.

He *was* bad news. Why did Theresa even care about him? He hurt her so much. Sure, he apologized, and he meant it, but she should've shoved his apology in his face and walked away.

The front door opened and closed. A gentle voice floated his way. He heard it, yet he barely understood the words coming out of her mouth.

"James?"

Jerking, he looked to his right to see his beautiful sister, her green eyes filled with concern.

"It's going to be okay. Why don't I—"

"Don't touch that bottle, Theresa." A deep wrenching pain stabbed him in the gut when he saw the hurt in her eyes with the way he snapped at her. "I won't open it."

Her expression turned stern, yet the concern still prominent in her gaze. "I don't believe you."

He looked at the bottle, his eyes glazing over.

"We can fight this. They can't fire you with no evidence. You didn't steal from them."

"I've stolen from you before. I'm bad news. What makes you think I didn't?"

Out of the corner of his eye, he saw her reach out to touch his shoulder and stop short of actually touching him. "Because I know you didn't. You didn't steal this time. You were in a bad place back then. You're not—"

"I think you should leave, Theresa." He kept his eyes straight ahead, unable to look at her and see the ache in her eyes.

"Maybe I should call—"

"Just go."

He didn't watch her retreat, her soft footsteps fading away, as his eyes zeroed in on the bottle. He should dump it down the sink.

Except he could do nothing but stand there and stare at it. Think about the terrible way he treated his sister when all she was trying to do was help.

Damn!

Swirling around from the bottle, he started inhaling deep breaths. One after another until a sliver of control slipped back in. Enough control to pull his phone out and call his sponsor, something Theresa had tried to tell him to do.

Fumbling with the screen, he finally managed to dial Terry.

He answered on the first ring.

"I need you. It's bad."

"Hang on, buddy. I'll be right there."

He disconnected, sliding the phone back in his pocket. He stood rooted in the same spot, his back to the bottle, until ten minutes later when Terry walked inside.

"What happened?"

James pressed his lips together as the anger, the rage, the all-consuming fury he lived with flared to life. Everyone always treated him like the bad seed of the town. Tried and hanged before he could even defend himself. Sure, Dr. Pearson asked if he had anything to say, and he could've claimed his innocence, but it wouldn't have changed the outcome.

"I got fired today from the hospital."

Terry nodded, his expression neutral. "Why's that?"

James couldn't even look him in the eye. "They think I was stealing drugs. You know, I'm an alcoholic, so of course I do drugs, too."

Terry scoffed, shaking his head. "And did you set them straight?"

He finally found the courage to look at him. "It wouldn't matter. It never does."

Nodding behind James to the bottle on the counter, Terry arched a brow. "And how does that help you? How does that fit into the scenario?"

"I couldn't stop myself." A strangled groan escaped. "I told my sister to leave. She was just trying to help. I hurt—"

Hell, he didn't want to talk about Erin. That almost hurt

more than hurting his sister. Because no matter how horrible he treated Theresa, he knew she'd always forgive him. He was an asshole for knowing that and using it to his advantage when he was pissed.

But Erin.

She wouldn't forgive him for walking out on her like he had. He didn't say anything bad to her, but it was the way he said goodbye. He basically told her to screw off.

And if she believed—like everyone else—that he stole those drugs, she *could* screw off. She was no better than anyone else. Of course she believed it. She tried to apologize to him before he walked out. She knew all along he was going to get fired.

"First things first, dump out the bottle."

A shiver rushed through his spine as he kept his gaze holding strong with Terry. "Can you do it for me?"

"Hell no. I didn't create the problem. You did. You fix it."

That was one thing he hated and loved about Terry. He was a hardass, no-nonsense kind of guy. He didn't coddle him. He didn't lie. He said everything straight and to the point. He said things he didn't always like to hear.

But it all helped him. It helped him stay on the right path.

He still wanted to punch the asshole in his face sometimes.

Terry walked over to the counter, snatched the Vodka bottle, and opened it. "You're strong, James. You're stronger than you give yourself credit for. You are a good man. You are a good person. You don't need this to make yourself feel better." Terry held the bottle out to him and then nodded at the sink. "Now repeat that to yourself and dump it out."

With trembling steps, he walked closer, took the bottle from Terry's outstretched hand, and stepped to the sink.

Hand trembling, he tipped the bottle over, aching for a sip as the liquor poured out in a steady stream.

"Say it, James. Believe it."

Blowing out a breath, he whispered, "I'm strong."

"Louder."

"I'm strong."

"Keep going."

"I'm a goo-good man."

"Say it again."

Inhaling a deep breath, his eyes mesmerized by the stream, he exhaled slowly. "I'm a good man."

"Keep going."

"I'm a good person."

"And?"

He shook the bottle when the stream died down, making sure every last drop escaped. "And I don't need this to make myself feel better."

"Damn right."

He slammed the bottle back on the counter, then turned toward Terry with a grin. "I still want a drink."

"Of course you do. So do I." Terry stepped closer and slapped him on the shoulder. "But we're strong." He squeezed his shoulder. "Your second step is to apologize to your sister. It'll make you feel better."

James nodded. "Yeah, maybe later."

Terry walked to the fridge and pulled out two bottles of water. "Let's go play some video games. I'm gonna kick your ass in that racing game this time." He held out a bottle of water. "Then you should be ready to apologize."

"I'm going to school you like I always do," he said with a laugh as he grabbed the bottle of water from his hand.

"We'll see. I've been practicing." Terry slapped his back again, urging him toward the living room. "Don't worry about what others think. You know the truth. You didn't steal anything. That's all that matters."

"You really believe that?"

Terry's eyes shimmered with honesty. "Yes, I do."

James sat down on the couch next to Terry, took a quick drink of water, then grabbed a controller.

He didn't care what others thought of him. If he did, he would've sunk to the bottom of the deep ocean way before now. The entire town could go screw themselves.

But damn. He did care what Erin thought.

That's what hurt the most.

He didn't want to care what she thought. He hated how much it gutted him that she thought he was a thief.

Glancing out the window at the gentle snow falling, he couldn't help but think of her and worry. Hopefully the snow didn't make the roads too bad tonight when she finished working her shift.

She wasn't his problem anymore.

She never was.

ERIN TRIED NOT to shiver from the blast of cold that rushed in with Daphne as she stepped through the automatic doors. Most of the time, she enjoyed working the front counter in the emergency room, directing patients to the appropriate area, calming family members down, answering questions, doing what she needed to do to maintain control. She ran this part of the hospital like a drill sergeant ran his platoon.

But sometimes she hated it. Especially when the weather outside was worsening by the minute. The wind, bustling around like a mad tornado, made everything worse every time someone walked inside. The snow was starting to take permanent residence outside on the sidewalk. Bob, one of the other janitors, had to switch his routine and shovel the snow outside a few times already.

James normally did it.

Forcing a smile out, she greeted Daphne as she approached the counter. Her eyes gazed down with a true smile as she stared at the white box wrapped with a red bow after Daphne set it on the counter.

"What's this?"

"It's nothing. Just a little Merry Christmas from me and Sean to you." Daphne pushed the box closer to her. "Honestly, it's not much."

Erin tried to think back through the last five years she had lived here, and she couldn't recall one time when Daphne hand-delivered a gift to her. They had never exchanged Christmas presents.

Her smile slowly died. She didn't quite wear a frown, nor did she look mad, just a neutral expression that would not relay what she was truly feeling.

Her gaze met Daphne's. "What's the occasion? I didn't know we were exchanging presents."

"No occasion. Sean and I wanted to give a few presents here and there. We're leaving a day early for the airport. We plan to spend the night in the Cities and then catch our flight tomorrow. The snow's starting to come down and we don't want to get stuck here and miss our flight."

Erin looked at the pretty white box again. A simple Christmas present. No way. She didn't think so.

Generally, she was a peacekeeper. She wore a friendly smile. She tried to keep patients and family members as calm as could be and as informed as they could be concerning their medical care.

Doing her job as friendly as possible was her motto. She had always believed in treating others as you wanted to be treated.

But sometimes, enough was enough.

Tearing her eyes away from the gift, she looked at Daphne, her expression still neutral. "I don't believe you."

Daphne looked taken aback, her hand jerking to her chest. "Did I do something wrong? What's the matter?"

Erin cocked her head to the side, eyeing Daphne quizzically. She knew Daphne was one of the nicest people in town, always willing to help someone out.

She was also one of the worst gossips in town. Maybe she didn't mean to come across as cruel, but that's how Erin pictured her right now. Cruel and vicious and without remorse for trying to dig out information about James so she could spread it like wildfire.

"You've never given me a present before, although I know you're a very kind person. But that's not your true motive in coming here, is it?"

Daphne's gaze fell, a light blush coating her cheeks. "I knew it'd be obvious." Her gaze snapped to hers. "I'm worried about you. I wanted to make sure you were okay."

This time, Erin was caught by surprise. "Excuse me? Why wouldn't I be okay?"

Daphne had the grace to look ashamed. "I know James was fired. I heard he stormed out of here yelling and making a fuss."

Erin's hands tightened into fists. "He left calmly and without a word. Whoever said that was lying."

"I figured she was embellishing a bit."

"She?" Erin rolled her eyes. "Let me guess. Marybeth."

Figures that nasty excuse for a human being would spread such lies about James. She suddenly hated Marybeth with a passion, and she couldn't remember a time when she actually hated another person.

"Yes, it was her. Are you okay?"

She was still confused. "Why wouldn't I be? I wasn't fired for something I didn't do."

Daphne smiled. At that moment, she finally understood what her friend Emma meant by Daphne's obnoxious trait of always smiling. She almost chuckled out loud remembering Emma talking about how annoying it could be and how it still grated on her nerves every time she saw Daphne.

She didn't go out as often as she liked, but on occasion, she went out with Emma and Theresa for some girl time. She only started to do that when James started working at the hospital and Theresa would visit him sometimes, bringing him lunch. One day, Theresa asked if she wanted to join them for game night at Emma's.

Daphne stood in front of her wondering how she was doing, but the better question was, how was Theresa doing?

"I know you've never said it, but I always thought... maybe..."

Erin's brow raised slightly. "Yes?"

"That you might like James. I wanted to stop in and see Theresa, and I tried at the diner, but she wasn't working today. So I thought I'd stop in and see how you're doing." Daphne shrugged, her bright smile still plastered on her face. "How is James doing?"

"James is only a friend. He was fired for something he didn't do, so I imagine he's upset. But I haven't spoken to him since he left."

By the glittering energy in Daphne's eyes, she didn't believe her lie. He was no friend. Well, he was her friend. At least, she hoped he still was.

But, yes, she did like him. From the first time he

walked up to the counter and smiled and said hello. His coffee-colored eyes had held her captivated, especially when he didn't simply look at her but it was as if he was devouring her with his gaze. His short beard, something she normally didn't care if a guy had on his face, had fascinated her. She had the strange urge to touch it, to smooth her hand across his jaw to see how rough—or even soft—it felt. And his classical brown hair. Always styled with a splash of flare. Smoothed back with finesse, yet with an air of messiness. Oh, yes, she definitely liked him from the start.

"I'm sorry if I upset you, Erin. That wasn't my intention."

Now Erin felt horrible for snapping at her. Smiling, a real one, not a fake one to appease her, she grabbed the box from the counter and set it on the desk in front of her. "Thank you, Daphne, for the gift. I hope you have a wonderful trip. Happy anniversary."

"Thank you. We're so excited to be going on a cruise." Daphne's eyes rounded with worry. "Please be careful driving."

"You, too." Erin glanced out the large bay windows, the night slowly descending, the snow falling down heavily. "Seriously, it looks like the snowstorm is getting worse by the minute."

Daphne smiled again, thanked her, apologized one more time, then left, letting in the brutally cold wind once more.

Erin shivered, and not just from the cold. James hated her. He thought she believed the horrible lies being spread about him. She would never believe he was a thief.

"Erin, Tonya's coming in early."

Jumping a little, her gaze connected with Dr. Pearson, who stood close to the counter. How did she not hear him walk up?

A gentle smile touched his lips. "I didn't mean to startle you."

"It's okay. Is she coming in early because of the snow?"

He nodded. "Yes, so when she gets here, please leave right away. I don't want you to get caught in it. Hopefully, it's not too busy tonight and people know better to stay off the roads. Drive safely, please."

"Of course. You, too, Dr. Pearson."

His smile never wavered as he nodded and then walked away. Not once did he bring up the way she talked to him earlier or how she hung up on him. Perhaps he knew he had been in the wrong to fire James. So why did he? What made them think James would steal drugs?

Ugh! It grated on her nerves. She wanted to find the real culprit. Start questioning every single employee until she found the right answer.

Except, she didn't have the courage to do so, and Tonya showed up ten minutes later. She said her goodbyes, grabbed the present she didn't bother to open yet and her purse, and headed for her car as the snow pelted her.

She didn't bother to race for her vehicle. The snow felt soothing. It didn't melt her anger for James, but it felt nice on her face.

By the time she made it home, the roads thick with snow, making it difficult to navigate, she was still upset by the events of the day.

She knew only one thing would make her feel marginally better.

Knowing how James was doing.

She couldn't go see him. That would be...odd. Out of character.

But she wanted to. She wanted to set the record straight. She wanted him to know he had a friend, if nothing else, from her. She might secretly like him, but she'd never have the courage to tell him.

Pulling the curtain to the side, she watched as the snow fell gracefully to the ground. It looked so serene and beautiful. Not like it was creating dangerous perils for anyone who dared to drive in it.

She had no reason to leave her house. She knew how terrible the roads were getting.

But James.

Every time she tried to think of something else, her mind circled back to him.

She had only one option.

She had to go see him.

Now.

During the start of a blizzard.

3

"Here. Take it."

James eyed the key dangling from Terry's hand. "I don't want it."

Terry nodded at the couch where they sat for three hours playing video games. His nerves had calmed somewhat and he didn't need a drink as badly as before, but his anger still consumed him. He needed at least twenty-four hours of game playing before he would be back in a mode where he could function without trembling for a drink. But the snow was coming down heavily, and Terry needed to hit the road before it became too bad and he was stuck here all night.

"We can only play so much. You should apologize to your sister, then take some time to yourself. My cabin is secluded. One road in, and one road out. I spend a lot of time there, so it's fully stocked with food and firewood and anything you might need." Terry tilted his head to the side. "When's the last time you took any time for yourself? You've worked so hard on your sobriety. You worked hard on finding a good job, a decent place to rent. All you've been doing for the past two years is work. Take the key, go to the cabin, and just relax. Put your feet up and enjoy the snow falling. It's a beautiful sight."

James followed Terry's gaze looking out the window to the snow steadily coming down. "Time to myself..."

"There's not a store in sight for miles. When I say you'll be secluded, you're secluded. And like I said before, it's stocked with plenty of food, tons of firewood to keep you warm, and," he smiled wide, "a gaming system. You won't have a chance to even think about wanting a drink. There's not one temptation in the cabin."

Being stuck in a cabin would make the cravings a lot easier. Right now with his anger ramped up to high levels, he needed to be far away from civilization. Maybe the cabin was the best solution.

Terry always knew the best thing for him, even when he didn't agree.

Reaching out, he took the key. "Fine. I'll stay one night."

"Stay as long as you'd like. You're spending Christmas Day with your sister, right?"

James nodded, unsure if he wanted to do that anymore. He'd be the pity party of the day, and that was the last thing he wanted. His sister wouldn't try to make it feel like that, but he'd feel it nonetheless.

"Then stay until Christmas if you want. Nobody will bother you. Especially if they don't know where you are."

A brow slowly rose. "Are you saying I shouldn't tell Theresa where I'm going?"

"No, of course not. You should tell her so she doesn't worry, but nobody else needs to know." Terry sighed. "The town doesn't need to know. I know how brutal the gossip can be sometimes." He stepped forward and slapped James' shoulder. "But it doesn't matter what anyone thinks. The truth always comes out."

"Not this time. I got fired and I didn't do a damn thing wrong."

"And eventually it'll bite them all in the ass." Terry squeezed his shoulder, then headed for his jacket hanging on a peg near the front door. "Head for Bookers Road, then take a right when you see a stick with a fish perched on the top. Follow it until the end. My cabin's right there."

"Bookers Road? Really? That's the last road to ever get plowed around here. And a fish on a stick?"

Terry chuckled, then a sadness touched his eyes. "My... my son used to love fishing. That's why I built it. He always loved that dumb fish sitting on a stick." Clearing his throat and avoiding eye contact, he slung his jacket on. "You better get going soon. You're right. That is the last road to be plowed because it's rarely used. The snow's coming down a lot heavier now and the fish might get buried. Reception's not that great out there, so it's not a guarantee you'll get service."

"I'll pack a bag and go. Don't worry about me."

Just like Terry wouldn't want him worrying about him. Terry didn't always talk about his son, but on the rare occasions he did, it made James feel better, as sad as that was. It meant he wasn't the only one suffering, that Terry had pain and heartache just as much as him. That when Terry gave advice, even if it was shit he didn't want to hear, he knew what he was talking about.

James knew his son died over twenty years ago, hit by a car playing in the yard. That's when Terry's path to alcohol and recovery started. Off and on he struggled, just like James. So if he thought time to himself, secluded away from other people, was the best thing right now, then he would listen.

"You're strong, James. You'll get through this like you've gotten through everything else."

A tiny smile emerged. "I hope to be as strong as you someday."

Terry winked, then opened the door. "Don't think I'm always strong, James. I repeat it daily in the mirror that I am. Have a good time. We haven't played that Zoomers game yet. I have it in the cabin. Practice up, otherwise, I'll school you in it."

"You're on."

Terry waved goodbye, then walked outside into the billowing cold, the snow blowing like the start of a tornado.

James packed a bag, throwing in several days' worth of clothes, grabbed his phone and his car keys, and headed outside. The snow struck him in the face immediately, sending chills down his spine. Shoving his knit cap lower, he dropped his shoulders and tried to shield his face from the cold wind as he traipsed through the heavy snow to his car.

Quite a bit had accumulated since he arrived home, but not enough where he thought he wouldn't be able to back out of his driveway. The plows looked like they came through his neighborhood already. They'd continue to do so throughout the night to attempt to stay ahead of the snow, throwing salt as they went.

He said a quick prayer his car would make it the small trek from his house to Theresa's, then to a small cabin deep in the woods.

The ride to Theresa's wasn't terrible, but it also wasn't completely pleasant. Some parts of the road had started to form snowdrifts on the side. The wind was constantly blowing and the plows, although were out full force, couldn't keep up as the snow continued to fall with a vengeance.

He needed to do this quickly before his car got stuck on his way to his destination. Hell, he might get stuck on the road leading to the cabin.

Jumping out of the car, head hanging low, he walked briskly to her door and knocked. A few seconds later, he stood face to face with the last person he wanted to see.

"*Officer Crowl.*"

Aiden, his sister's husband, raised his brow. "Oh, we're back to talking to each other that way, Brennen?"

James immediately felt like an asshole, but the words of apology wouldn't reach his lips. He shrugged instead. "Well, you're a cop. I'm a criminal."

Aiden rolled his eyes and shoved a hand around his shoulder, pulling him inside. "You made my wife cry, so I'm tempted to hit you right now." His arm around his shoulder tightened, almost like a hug, as the door shut behind them. "But I get why you're acting like this. I'm sorry to hear about your job."

"And that I had to steal," James scoffed, dislodging his arm from around his shoulder.

Aiden stopped walking, blocking his path to his sister, wherever she was in the house. "I don't think you stole anything. You're an asshole. You're difficult to deal with sometimes. But I know you've been working hard on changing your life."

He felt like he had just been punched straight in the gut, all the air whooshing out, struggling to breathe. Aiden's words didn't sound false or even forced. He said it like he believed it.

"I didn't mean to make Theresa cry."

Aiden nodded. "She knows why you made her leave. Doesn't mean she liked it."

"Do you know?"

A hard glare entered Aiden's eyes. "I do, and if you're going to make her cry again, I'm going to have to ask you to leave."

"I was in a bad place, Offic—Aiden." Just because the anger was consuming him to the point of madness didn't mean he had to revert to his assholish ways. The guy wasn't all that bad. He treated his sister right, so there was that. But he was also a cop, and he never liked cops. And he was, back in the day, part of the in-crowd that never gave him or his sister the time of day.

"And now? Where are you at?"

James shrugged. "I don't know. Stuck in the middle, but I'm trying to find my way back. I need some time to myself, but I wanted to see Theresa first."

The worry he'd upset Theresa again started to dissipate from Aiden's eyes. "She's in the living room." Aiden started leading the way, then stopped and turned his way. "I know we don't always get along, but we're family. As much as it pains you." A wily smirk touched his lips. "I'm sure it pains you a lot." They both chuckled. "But we're here for you. Both of us. Don't ever forget that."

Before he could respond, not sure how he should, Aiden walked away. James headed for the living room as he watched Aiden veer toward the kitchen. The second Theresa saw him, she jumped up from the couch and approached him.

Since she looked hesitant, he held out his arms, letting her know it was okay to hug him. Because sometimes, when he had a bad moment, he didn't like to be touched. She sunk into his embrace, tightening her arms around him.

"I'm sorry, Tessy. I didn't mean to act like a dick."

"You have nothing to be sorry about."

"Don't let me get away with shit. You know I shouldn't have treated you that way."

She lifted her head and smiled. "You were upset, and rightly so. The only apology I want to hear is the one from the hospital to you."

A strangled laugh came out as she let go and took a step away. "Good luck with that."

"Maybe Aiden should—"

"Mind his business. I don't want him acting all cop-like and digging into anything. Leave it be."

Theresa frowned. "But they fired you with lies."

Thinking about what happened earlier only made the anger inside him burn like an out-of-control forest fire. It also made him think of Erin and how he wouldn't get to see her beautiful emerald green eyes and her sweet smile, or hear her witty conversations every day. That hurt more than losing his job.

It hurt even more that she thought he was a thief.

"It's done, Theresa. I don't want to keep talking about it." His expression softened. "Please."

A smile lit up her face. "We're going to watch a movie and have some popcorn and hot chocolate. Do you want to spend the night and hang out with us?"

He knew she was only trying to help, to make him feel better and like he was a part of the family, but no matter how hard she tried, he always felt like an outsider. He probably always would. She found a good man to build a good life with. But him? He didn't see himself ever settling down with a wife and kids with a white picket fence. Hanging around his sister too much might get his hopes up he could have the same thing. To protect himself, he tried to stay away as much as possible but also coming around just enough where she wouldn't worry too much about him.

"It's a nice offer, but Terry said I could go relax in his cabin. I need some time to myself. I took him up on the offer."

"On Bookers Road, right?"

Why was he surprised his sister knew that? Since marrying Aiden, she was always in the know about most things around town, including people's lives.

"Yeah, that one." He offered a grin to lessen what she might consider an insult. "Don't tell anyone, though. I don't want anyone bugging me."

Including you were his unspoken words.

"Be careful driving. The snow is getting worse."

Yeah, which meant he needed to wrap this up. "I thought Aiden usually worked nights. Why isn't he out there?"

Theresa shivered, concern lighting her eyes. "Chief Duncan called him and said to stay home. He doesn't expect many people on the roads, so he reduced the staff for the evening. Although, he is on-call if they need him."

He pulled Theresa in for another hug. "Be safe, too. Stay home."

She squeezed him hard. "We'll see you on Christmas."

He kissed the top of her head but said nothing in return. He didn't want to disappoint her. Because he wasn't sure he would be seeing her on Christmas. If he couldn't sort out his emotions, control his anger, then he didn't want to be around anyone, especially his sister. He didn't want to ruin her Christmas.

After a quick goodbye to Aiden, he waved goodbye as they both watched him from the doorway and drove away.

He took his time driving, the visibility getting worse, his car swerving and fishtailing a few times. The minute he turned on Bookers Road, everything, including the road, turned to shit. Not wanting to spiral into the ditch, he slowed down to almost a crawl. Even driving as slowly as he was, he almost missed the fish on the stick. Not because it was almost completely covered and barely sticking out of the snow, but because the snow was coming down so strong and hard it was difficult to see two inches in front of him. The pitch-black night didn't help either.

He got about a block down what he figured was a dirt road, but couldn't tell with the snow building, before his tires started spinning.

Great. He was stuck.

Squinting, he leaned closer to the wheel, looking out into the dark, snowy night.

Well, he wasn't going anywhere with his car stuck. So, if he didn't want to freeze to death, he'd have to make the rest of the walk on foot.

Grabbing his duffle bag from the passenger seat, he exited the car, stuck his hands in his pockets, bent his head, and started walking.

Maybe the cold, brutal air with the snow pelting his face would tame his anger.

Because as he put one foot in front of the other, it hurt like hell, sending shiver after shiver down his spine, but it also felt good. It felt refreshing.

It felt like he had no care in the world but to find warmth and some solitude.

4

SHOULDERS HUNCHED, head tucked in, bundled from head to toe in her snow gear, she knocked on James' door again. She knew it was futile to keep knocking, but she couldn't help trying one more time.

Ugh! He wasn't going to answer. The lights were out. He wasn't home.

Where did he go?

Huffing out a breath, she twirled around on his step, almost losing her balance from the snow piling. Straightening her stance, she took her time but with a slight pep in her step as she went back to her car.

Immediately turning the car on, the heat rushing out on full blast, she rubbed her gloved hands together.

He wasn't home.

Where would he go after being fired, and with a blizzard on the way? It was a harder question to answer than she imagined.

The most logical answer would be Theresa's, but what if she was wrong? She wasn't sure she was ready to admit to anyone that she liked James more than a friend. And to his sister? Awkward.

But her and Theresa were friends. It wouldn't be so odd for her to inquire about James because she was also friends with him.

She stared out her windshield, watching as the snow gracefully fell. Since she was a child, she always loved the snow. Playing with her sister outside, taking walks while it snowed all around her, watching it accumulate until there was enough to build a snowman. She would even admit to eating it, as long as it didn't look yellow. The snow was always a beautiful sight to her.

Driving in it was a disaster waiting to happen, though. Finding out if James was okay was important, but not so important if she got into an accident and hurt herself. The roads, although being steadily plowed, were still difficult to maneuver.

A slight shiver rushed up her spine, even as the heat was starting to warm her up. Pulling off her gloves, the extra warm pair she owned, she grabbed her phone from her purse and dialed Theresa's number before she could change her mind.

"Hey, Erin."

"Hi, so sorry to bother you." She inhaled a breath, wondering how to proceed. With honesty? With a bit of pretense?

"Is everything okay?"

A flashback of Daphne walking up to her counter with a present in her hand had her going with honesty. She didn't appreciate Daphne's underhanded way of gathering information. She still hadn't opened the gift from her.

"I'm sitting in James' driveway. I've been worried about him since he left. I wanted to make sure he's okay. If he's with you, then..." Well, then she couldn't be with him. As long as he was okay, that's what mattered. "Then that's good. I just wanted to make sure he's okay."

And now she was repeating herself. She sounded like a complete idiot.

"He's not here."

Her heart started to race. Where was he, then? Maybe he got hurt driving in the snow. Maybe he—

"But he stopped by."

A breath escaped that she hadn't realized she started holding.

"He's not okay, Erin. He got fired for something he didn't do."

Her bottom lip started to tremble. She could not lose it over the phone with his sister. She absolutely could not.

"I know. I tried to talk to him before he left. I tried to..." Thinking about it now, saying sorry was the dumbest thing she could've said to him. Of course he would think she knew everything and believed it all by saying sorry. What did you say to someone who got fired, though? Unjustly fired, at that.

"You're a good friend, Erin. It's nice knowing you're worried about him. I haven't had anyone else call, well, besides Emma and Lynn, but I knew they would." Theresa sighed. "It means a lot that you reached out."

It was her turn to sigh. Should she admit how much she cared about him? That she had a silly crush on him like she was back in high school.

It had been so long since she dated. Five years, to be exact. She hadn't dated anyone in this small town. A small town that sometimes grated on her nerves with their nosiness.

"So, he's okay? I mean, not okay okay, but okay?"

Banging her head lightly on the steering wheel, she wanted to groan out loud at her idiocy. Maybe she should hang up because every word out of her mouth sounded stupid. How many times could she say the word *okay*? Theresa already said he wasn't okay.

Sweet, light laughter echoed in her ear. "He's better than he was when he first left, if that's what you mean." She paused. "He told me not to tell anyone where he went. He wanted some time to himself."

"Right. Okay." She internally screamed at repeating that damn word again. "That's good to hear. I'm glad he's—" Suddenly crazy laughter wanted to escape. "Fine."

Theresa obviously couldn't hold in the laughter. "You so wanted to say *okay* again."

Erin started to laugh with her. "I did."

Theresa's laughter slowly died down. She wouldn't call it an awkward silence, but silence hung between them.

"If..."

Erin's heart pounded like someone was hammering hard against her chest. "Yeah?"

"If I tell you where he is, what will you do with that information?"

Her heart sped up double-time as if that hammer wouldn't stop until it made a huge dent that couldn't be fixed. What would she do with that information? Theresa already assured her he was...well, okay. Did she still need to see him? What would she say to him? She was losing her mind and couldn't manage to speak properly. Was it the best time to confront him?

Confront wasn't the right word. That seemed to denote there was something wrong between them.

But wasn't there? He thought she knew he was getting

fired. He thought she believed Dr. Pearson that he was a thief.

"Erin?"

Right. She needed an answer.

"I hate to bother him...if he doesn't want any visitors."

"Maybe he'd be...receptive to one."

Erin wasn't so sure he would be.

"It would be nice to see he was okay for myself." She laughed as she said *okay* for the billionth time.

"And you won't tell anyone else where he is?"

She was almost offended Theresa asked such a question. Because when it came to gossip around town, she stayed far away from it.

But she wasn't hurt. Because Theresa was only looking out for her brother.

"Of course not."

Theresa let out a big breath.

"He's staying in Terry's cabin on Bookers Road. As soon as you see a fish on top of a stick, take that right and follow the road until the end."

Sounded easy enough. Not that she ventured on that road very often, but how hard could it be to see a fish on a stick?

Glancing out the window at the pretty snowfall, she realized it might be harder than she anticipated.

"Thanks, Theresa. I appreciate it."

"Yeah, well, he might not be too happy I told you, so... just be aware that he might be...not in a good mood."

"Then why'd you tell me? I guess I don't understand."

Theresa's voice dropped to a whisper. "Because I want my brother to be happy. And I think he could be with you. Or am I seeing things wrong?"

Erin bit her bottom lip as a smile wanted to break free.

Apparently, she didn't hide her crush on James as well as she thought.

"I think your eyesight is fine. Thanks."

"You're welcome." Theresa paused, a hint of concern mingled in with her next words. "If you're driving to see him tonight, well, maybe you should wait. The roads are getting worse by the second. Aiden was just called into work because they've had quite a few more calls of people getting stuck than Chief Duncan anticipated."

"I'll be okay." There was that dumb word again. "I'm at James' house, remember? I still have to drive home. But you're right, maybe I'll wait until tomorrow to go see him."

"Drive safely, Erin."

She thanked Theresa again, then hung up.

Eyeing the glistening snow, the night twinkling all around, she knew as much as she shouldn't, she had a destination in mind.

And it wasn't home.

She couldn't describe the intense feeling that she had to see him tonight. That she had to apologize right now.

She knew it was the right thing to do.

Backing out of his driveway slowly, she tried to ignore the warning bells of her decision.

It would be okay.

Everything would be okay.

If she repeated that stupid word over and over, she might start to believe it.

RUBBING his hands together near the fire, he finally had to admit—because he had a hard time admitting while trudging through the snow—this was a good idea by Terry.

It was quiet here, peaceful, in a way he hadn't experienced in...ever. He couldn't recall a time he had felt peace. His mind was always racing with what task he had to tackle next. Even before he got sober, his mind used to race when he could start drinking again. His mind never shut off.

But here, in the woods, the quiet, the peace, no one around for miles, he found he had no care in the world. His mind didn't need to be in overdrive. He had no pressing concerns. Hell, how could he? He had no job anymore.

He wouldn't be able to drink because there was no liquor in the cabin and no store in sight. Since winding down with Terry and the long trek through the snow, his urge to have a drink had significantly lessened. He was starting to get back to the stable equilibrium that he worked on daily to maintain.

Standing up from the fireplace, his eyes mesmerized by the flames burning bright, he was glad he had no cell service. Not even his sister could call him to check on him.

That was a terrible thing to want, but this peace he managed to claim for himself, he wanted to indulge in it as long as he could. Because when he left, when his time was up, all that worry, all that anxiety would come rushing back in. He'd be right back where he was before he left.

That walk through the snow had done more than just help him admit Terry was right. It cleared his mind. Oh, the winter storm held so many wonders. The bite of wind hitting his cheeks. The wet snow seeping into his shoes making his feet freeze. The brutal temperatures burrowing deep into his bones. It also managed to set his life in perspective.

When he left this cabin, he was leaving for good.

This town did nothing for him.

Even as a kid growing up, he was always the odd man

out. The white trash that lived in the shitty part of town. Theresa always seemed to be able to brush it off and ignore what others thought, living in her own little bubble. Him, on the other hand, he let his anger get the best of him. Getting into fights at school, smoking pot, drinking. Hell, he even snatched candy and chips from the convenience store a few times. They never caught him.

His childhood sucked. His dad constantly drank. His mom pretended life was okay. All that shittiness he endured at home transferred to school.

Then he met Dusty, and from there, as they say, it all went downhill. It took that asshole lighting his sister's house on fire to snap him out of it. To get his life on a decent track.

Every day was a struggle.

Every day, living in the gossipy town, was a struggle.

Every day, saying hi to Erin, talking to her, knowing he could never have something as pure and sweet as her, was a damn struggle.

He was done struggling.

He was leaving. Heading out for a new place, a new home, a new adventure.

Of course, he needed to keep his sobriety because otherwise he'd be trading an old hell for a new one. Terry should be able to help him find a new sponsor, one as strong and hardheaded, yet compassionate when he needed them to be. That's what he needed. He needed a drill sergeant, but with a touch of gentleness. He liked how Terry treated him. It'd be hard to find a replacement.

But he had no choice. Because Terry wouldn't follow him, and he would never ask him to do that.

He couldn't stay in this shitty-ass town anymore. Not after getting fired for something he didn't do. All that hard work. All that focus and determination to show everyone he could be better. It was all for nothing.

"Bunch of assholes."

Shaking his head, he tried to let go of the negativity and turned around to find something to eat.

It was a small cabin. Enough space for a single guy who liked some time to himself. Hunt a little. Fish a little. Although he hadn't known exactly where Terry's cabin was before now, he knew he liked to hunt and fish. He figured there had to be a lake or small pond nearby where he fished, especially when he used a silly fish on a stick as a landmark.

Well, no, it wasn't silly. It was a reminder of his son. The one he lost.

Crossing through the tiny living room to the kitchen, he started opening and closing cupboards to see what he had available. And boy, Terry hadn't lied when he said it was stocked. He had his choice of pickings from canned soap to making a hot dish if he wanted. He knew how to cook, he just didn't normally put forth the effort.

He either nuked TV dinners in the microwave for supper, or his sister dropped off a variety of meals on any given day. Sometimes she insisted he come over and join them for a meal. He didn't particularly like those times, but he did it. For her.

His hand tightened around a nob as he stared inside the cupboard, zoning out, thinking how much he'd miss his sister when he left. She was his rock. Even through all the hard times, she was always there. It would be damn hard leaving her.

Slamming the cupboard door closed, he took a step back, breathing heavily. Large gulps of air as if he had taken a hard punch to the gut.

He had to leave. He had no choice. If he wanted to keep

this sense of peace he found, he needed to leave. There was no other option.

Glancing around the tiny cabin, eyeing the drab couch sitting in the middle of the living room, to the small table near the front window, to the fireplace all lit up, flames dancing brightly, he wasn't sure what he should do next. Go to bed? Maybe he could sleep off the rest of the anguish still swimming through his veins. From the spot he was standing in the kitchen, he could even see the short hallway, if one could even call it that. Not more than two feet from the living room were two doors. One door led to the bedroom, the other door on the opposite side was to the bathroom. That's it. That's how tiny the cabin was, and he loved it.

The small space didn't make him feel confined at all, not like he thought it might when he first stepped inside.

He was going to enjoy the next few days here. And it would be a few days, considering his car was stuck and the snow was falling pretty heavily. It'd be a few days before the plows even made it out this way.

Which was fine by him. He didn't need or want anyone bugging him.

He was fine by himself.

Pulling open a different cupboard, he grabbed a box of cereal, then got some milk, a bowl, and a spoon. It might not be much of a supper, but it'd do for now.

He was hungry, and he needed something to occupy his mind other than worrying about his future and the thought of leaving.

Because he wouldn't just miss his sister.

He'd miss Erin, too.

God, he'd miss her. The first woman who ever captured his attention.

Why should he miss her? She believed he was a thief.

She didn't even give him a heads up he was about to be fired. What kind of friend was that?

Clearly, she wasn't. Never had been.

Despite all that, he'd miss her.

He paused, his spoon inches from his mouth when the lights flickered. He'd been lucky when he reached the cabin, unlocking it without any issues, the lights springing on without a problem. He struggled making a fire, but he eventually got it started. The electricity was working, and the heat, with the added fire, was working. The tiny cabin was a good escape.

But if the power went out, so would his heat. Sure, he had the fire going, a big pile of firewood in the corner, but that wouldn't keep him completely warm. He wouldn't be able to survive out here like that. He was no outdoorsman. He could fully admit he'd be like a fish out of water if the power went out.

The lights flickered again as he shoved the spoonful of cereal into his mouth, then chewed slowly.

He could only say a little prayer that the power would stay strong. Because honestly, he couldn't take many more surprises in his life.

5

SLOWING DOWN, although she was already driving at a snail pace, a smile curved her lips when she saw something sticking out of a snowdrift on the right side of the road. It was hard to tell exactly what it was with the snow blowing everywhere. Everything was pitch black, too, but based on the shape she could somewhat make out, she thought it was a fish.

She found her turn. Finally!

She took the turn wide, not wanting to drive into the ditch, because at this point it was hard to tell where the road ended and the ditch started.

On a scale of one to complete idiocy, she was gearing toward the complete idiocy spectrum for even attempting to see him tonight. When people walked in injured, especially for driving in bad weather, she always looked at them with wonderment. Why didn't they have the common sense to stay at home?

That same question could be applied to her right now.

Except she kept forging on, inching her car forward in snow so deep she was surprised she hadn't gotten stuck yet.

She didn't get very far before she had no choice but to stop when a car sat in her path. It looked like James' vehicle.

With her car still running, she hopped out. Yanking on his door handle, it wouldn't budge. She pressed closer to the window, cupping her hands around her face as she peered inside.

Empty.

A rush of air escaped. Her heart slowed its crazy pitter-patter of terror when she thought he had gotten in an accident.

Stepping back, she looked ahead. The snow swirled around, the wind whipping, cold and brutal.

In all likelihood, he got stuck, which meant she would've eventually as well.

Walking back to her car, she rubbed her hands together, trying to warm up from the short stint in the cold. She had barely been outside for less than two minutes and she felt frozen to the bone.

She had two choices.

Back up and go home, wait for a better time to see him.

Or get out and start walking toward the cabin.

"This is silly, Erin. What were you thinking?"

Dropping her head to the steering wheel, a pained breath released. If she got out and walked—and for how long, she didn't know—to reach him, he wouldn't want to see her.

He hated her.

The disgust in his whispered tone as he said goodbye said enough. The hurt in his eyes, the tragic way he walked out with his shoulders slumped, said enough.

He wouldn't want to see her.

She was foolish to think he would.

Decision made, she put the car in reverse and pressed

her foot to the gas. The wheels spun, grinding noises echoing around outside, but she didn't move. She kept pressing, a little harder each time, until she knew it was futile.

She was officially stuck.

Laying her forehead on the steering wheel once again, laughter spilled out this time.

Well, he might hate her, but he'd have to deal with her.

She had nowhere else to go.

Grabbing the light duffle bag she packed before leaving, prepared for any kind of scenario with this kind of weather, she turned the car off, locked the door, and started walking.

There was no sign of James' footprints. They were obviously replaced with new snow; it was coming down even heavier than before. She had no good path to follow or any way to tell if she was even going in the right direction. The only thing that gave her hope she was walking toward the cabin was the trees lining both sides. And thank goodness for those trees, otherwise she would've been screwed. Because, besides the tall looming beauty of nature, it was a whiteout. A white blanket of magical glory everywhere she looked.

Even freezing as she took one step after another, the snow pelting her face, making her shiver as she continued, it was beautiful. If she wouldn't turn into an icicle, she would've loved to sit down, lay back, and watch the snow fall all around her.

But she couldn't.

Because, although she dressed in her warmest snow gear, minus snow pants, the cold was seeping through and freezing her to the core.

One foot in front of the other. She kept repeating it as she walked.

What she should've been thinking about was what she would say to James when she knocked on the door.

I'm sorry sounded like the best thing to start with.

AFTER HELPING AN OLDER gentleman to room five with a nasty gash on his forehead, Aiden took a deep breath and tried to get his head into police mode.

But it was hard. Theresa was home alone, most likely feigning watching a Christmas movie, but in reality worrying like crazy about her brother.

When Chief Duncan called him needing his help, Aiden couldn't say no. Chief Duncan hadn't anticipated so many people being on the roads. People probably thought the snowstorm wouldn't turn this bad so fast.

Aiden was a little surprised himself. One minute it was falling gently, almost serenely, and the next, the wind was whipping, the snow coming down like a running waterfall.

He'd only been out in the streets for an hour and he had already helped three cars get unstuck. He even stopped to help Bentley, who was also called in by the fire department, get a truck out of the ditch.

The latest accident, the old man sitting in the driver's seat hit his head so hard on the steering wheel, he wouldn't be surprised if he suffered a concussion. Not knowing how long it'd take for an ambulance to arrive, he had helped the gentleman in his car and drove him to the emergency room himself.

Heading for the exit, he almost ran right into Dr. Pearson as he turned the corner. A smile lit up Dr. Pearson's face.

"Hello, Aiden. I hear we have some potential stitches in room five."

"Yep. Maybe a concussion, too." A frown appeared, almost an evil sneer twisted his lips. "But you're the doc. You know better than me."

Dr. Pearson looked taken aback, even took a step away from him as the words flew out of his mouth harshly.

He hadn't meant for his words to sound so severe, but he couldn't help it. His wife was home alone, insanely worried about her brother, and it was all because of this man. No matter how much he might not like James at times, he didn't believe he stole a damn thing from the hospital, let alone drugs.

"Everything okay, Aid—Officer Crowl?"

Interesting. Dr. Pearson understood the malice behind his words. He immediately reverted from a friendly buddy —not that they were buddies—to professional.

"Everything's fine. Other than a snowstorm we haven't seen in quite a few years. And you?"

Aiden wasn't sure why he even asked. He couldn't care less about how he was feeling. Was he feeling guilty for firing an innocent man? Was he feeling regret? Was he feeling an ounce of remorse?

Yeah, he cared about those questions. He wanted answers. But any other feelings Dr. Pearson might have, he didn't give a shit.

Because nobody made his wife cry and didn't see his wrath.

James was her brother. As much as it pained him when James was acting like an ass, that made him his brother, too.

And he always stuck by his family.

"It's been a busy and...a trying day." Dr. Pearson inhaled deeply, then exhaled, a morose expression touching his face. "You're upset about James. I know he's your brother-in-law, but—"

Aiden held up his hand. "Don't. I know James a lot better than you do. I don't always see eye to eye with him, but he's my family. And he's no damn thief." His lips thinned, his brows burrowing low with a menacing glare. "There might be a helluva storm going on out there, but it hasn't seemed to slow down the gossip. I keep hearing everything about how everyone knew he was no good. How they knew he couldn't keep a decent job. How surprised they were to know he kept his job for as long as he did." His eyes narrowed. "What I haven't heard is how they know he stole anything. How do you know? Because I don't believe for one damn second he stole any drugs."

Dr. Pearson's entire stance stiffened. "We have a witness. They saw him in the act."

"Who's your witness?"

Dr. Pearson swallowed hard. "I'd rather not say."

Aiden shifted his weight, placing a hand on his waist near his weapon. Not that he planned to pull it out or anything, but sometimes it made people nervous thinking he might. Dr. Pearson was no exception. His eyes rounded, yet he said nothing.

"I don't believe a police report was filed. You say you have a witness, something you're oddly not wanting to divulge. Why aren't you charging James?"

"We thought it was best to let him go and move on. He was a good worker. He made a mistake, but I do hope the best for him."

Aiden leaned closer, his voice dripping with venom. "You're full of shit, Dr. Pearson, and so is your witness." He backed away, stood tall, dropped his hand, and produced a smile. "Have a good night."

Walking around Dr. Pearson, he knew he couldn't let this slide. It wasn't right that James was being attacked for something he didn't do. He also knew he couldn't keep standing there talking to him, otherwise, he was liable to do something stupid. Like hit the man.

All he could see standing there was Theresa, the sad look in her eyes as she cried explaining everything to him. The way James looked hurt and broken, like he couldn't take another blow or he'd succumb to every single beating life threw at him.

Yeah, the guy made mistakes. But he paid for them. He worked hard every day to set his life on a good path, especially with the help from Theresa, and even him.

He didn't believe he stole any drugs. He believed in James, even before he spoke to him today.

After shutting his car door, immediately turning it on and blasting the heat, he pulled out his phone.

"Hey, Chief. We need to talk about James Brennen. Something's up about...well, everything that happened today. Him getting fired and the reason why. Will you help me?"

ERIN COULD ADMIT, maybe not to anyone else if they asked, that she loved the snow, but she hated the cold. She especially hated the cold while walking in single-digit temperatures as the snow whipped and swirled around. Trudging through the snow—at least a foot tall, if not more—heading toward what she hoped was the cabin, was not easy.

Trees lined her path, so she figured she wasn't walking in the wrong direction, but she had yet to see anything. Not even a sliver of light.

She had no idea how long she had been walking. Maybe ten minutes. Maybe thirty. It all felt like hours to her. Her hands, although covered in thick winter gloves, were frozen to the bone, even tucked inside her large winter coat. She had on a heavy knit maroon hat and a rainbow-colored scarf wrapped around her neck and mouth. The only thing visible right now were her eyes, and she desperately wished she would've grabbed goggles or something to shield her eyes from the brutal wind.

Snow pants never crossed her mind. Her legs were only covered with jeans, but she did think to put on long johns underneath for an extra layer of warmth. Her heavy-duty snow boots were tied tightly on her feet. No snow had fallen inside, but they were still frozen to the bone.

Even as cold as she felt, like an icicle dangling from the gutters of a magnificent home, the night was beautiful. The snow, harsh and cruel, was still a gorgeous sight. She never got sick of watching the snow fall; she just preferred to watch it fall from inside a nice warm building.

Concentrating on putting one foot in front of the other, she didn't have time to contemplate what to say to James. What could she say other than she was sorry? Which was what she tried to tell him when he walked out of the emergency room.

She was sorry.

She was sorry that they treated him so unfairly.

She was sorry that nobody asked her any questions about this supposed theft. She would've told them right away she didn't think he did it.

She was sorry she couldn't offer him any sort of comfort at all. A hand on the shoulder in support. A quick hug. A tiny kiss.

Oh, now *that* was wishful thinking on her part.

Growing up, boys had never been her strong suit. More like her good buddies. She played all kinds of sports with them, mostly basketball in the community center close to her house. She even dabbled a bit with skateboarding, but she was never very good at it.

But flirting. That never came into play. Boys were easy to talk to about sports, school, and non-girly things, but she never tried to flirt with any of them. Some people even called her a tomboy on occasion. The title never bothered her. Because it fit her. That's not to say she didn't hang out with girls, too. She hung out with everyone.

She talked to her best friend, Bethany, at least once a month, sometimes once a week, since moving away from her hometown close to the Cities. Bethany still hung out with a few people they associated with in college, one of them being her ex-boyfriend Tommy.

As a swift shiver rushed up her spine at a strong gust of wind, she almost paused in her walking when it hit her.

Even though they considered each other boyfriend and girlfriend, it was more like a boy and girl...that were friends. Okay, with some benefits on the side. They had sex. They watched movies and went out to eat together. They played basketball on the weekends. But they didn't dig deep. They didn't have a strong emotional connection.

Erin figured if they would've had that, he would've considered moving with her, or at least continued the relationship at a distance.

She missed Tommy. She missed his friendship. But she wouldn't say she missed him as a boyfriend.

James, on the other hand...

Just thinking about never seeing him again. Talking to him again. It was like an arrow pierced her heart and twisted and kept twisting until it was disengaged, leaving nothing but a mangled piece in shreds.

It was crazy. They didn't do anything outside of work.

Chit-chatted before he started his shift and a little bit of conversation before he left. Nine months of simple talking and she knew she'd miss him more than she missed her ex-boyfriend that she dated for three years in college.

A tiny circle appeared in the distance. A white circle.

A light. Not a circle. A bright, warm light peeking out of a small window.

The thought of warmth, of sitting by a fire—if she was lucky—forced her to increase her pace. And like a miracle sent from heaven, she was within twenty feet of a small cabin decked out with a short porch, just enough room to fit a bench.

Her steps slowed.

She was freezing, maybe to the point of hypothermia. Okay, probably a little exaggeration on her part, but she was bone-deep cold.

Yet, she walked like a snail, taking her time to the front door.

What would she say?

Better yet, what would he say?

Well, James wasn't a cruel man, he wouldn't turn her away. He'd let her in. Let her warm up.

But would he accept her apology? Could they go back to their easy camaraderie? Could they still be friends and hang out even if he didn't work at the hospital anymore?

Only one way to find out.

Moving faster, she walked right up to the door and knocked loudly. No hesitation. No thinking about his reaction.

Shivering, more than she had when she had been walking, she wondered if she didn't knock hard enough. She thought she had. But why wasn't he answering?

Raising her gloved fist again, she swung it forward,

nearly tripping on her feet when the door swung open. Losing her balance from the surprise, her fist knocked into his chest instead of the door.

James caught her around the waist, holding her steady.

The shock in his eyes mesmerized her. A mixture of confusion, surprise, and amazement.

"Erin? What..." His brows puckered low. "What are you doing here?"

That long treacherous walk she just completed, she had all the time in the world to come up with something good to say.

And now, nothing. No words came out. Not even her apology she wanted to offer.

Although she couldn't feel anything through her large winter coat, his soft touch, his sweet hands on her waist, was rendering her speechless.

She had never been in his arms before. Not even in a small hug.

Right now, right here in this moment, she wanted to be completely in his arms. She wanted to close the distance and soak up his warmth, his kindness, his sweetness. Let him know in that one big gesture how much she cared about him. Because no matter what anyone said or thought about him, he was a sweet, kind, thoughtful man.

When was the last time someone other than his sister told him how important he was in their life?

Without a word, she dropped her fist from his chest, stepped forward and wrapped her arms around him.

JAMES DIDN'T KNOW what to do, except stand there and soak up how wonderful it felt to have Erin in his arms. He never thought he'd get to experience it. She was so out of his league and—

And she thought he was a thief.

What was going on? Why was she here? How did she even know he'd be here?

Stiffening, he heard her inhale sharply. He stepped away and let his arms drop from around her waist, not caring how enticing and right it felt to hold her. He took another step back for safe measure and her hands fell away from him. The sad, dejected look in her eyes almost crumbled his resolve. He wanted to pull her back into his embrace because he couldn't take the pain in her eyes.

"You better come inside before all the heat escapes." His jaw tightened when she winced at his harsh tone.

With a duffle bag slung over one shoulder, all bundled up in snow gear, she stepped inside the very tiny—maybe way too tiny—cabin.

As soon as she closed the door, he knew this cabin would not be big enough for both of them. But he'd have no choice but to let her stay the night. By the way the snow clung to the bottom of her jeans, her rosy red cheeks, and the shivers coating her body, she walked to the cabin as he had. Well, duh. Of course, she had. His car was parked in the middle of the road leading to the cabin.

"Thanks." Her mouth slightly curved into a smile. A hesitant one.

"Didn't have a choice." He turned around, stalking to the kitchen.

He hated that miserable look in her eyes. He hated the way he just spoke to her. He hated...God, he hated how much he wanted to have her back in his arms.

But he couldn't. Not when she believed he was a thief.

"James...I..."

Whipping open a cupboard, he stared hard at all the contents, figuring out what to pull out. He had to grab something, otherwise, he'd look like an idiot. Like he ran away from her instead of walking away with a purpose. The truth was he walked away because he *was* running. He didn't know what to say. Only hateful, spiteful things wanted to spew out, and no matter how much Erin believed he stole from the hospital, he didn't want to take his anger out on her.

The longer he stared, the more confused he became at what to grab.

He trembled when a soft hand touched his shoulder. Yet, he didn't turn her way.

"I don't think you stole anything. Earlier today...when you were leaving..."

His eyes closed as her hand tightened on his shoulder.

"I was trying to say I'm sorry about the way they treated you."

Opening his eyes, his gaze leveled on the only thing that made sense. Grabbing the box of hot chocolate, he turned around, missing her soft touch immediately when she dropped her hand from his shoulder.

"You should take off your jacket, put your boots by the fire, grab a blanket and warm up. I'll make some hot chocolate. That should help, too."

Her mouth opened as if she wanted to say more about the hospital, but she smiled instead, one of her sweet smiles he always loved seeing, then nodded. "I am freezing. That sounds like a great idea."

He headed for the fridge to grab some milk while he heard her unzip her jacket. Focusing hard on his task, he tried like hell not to look at her. He couldn't believe she was there. Did he even want to know how she found him? Or why?

Why did she drive out here? Walk in the middle of a blizzard? Just to see him? He was a nobody. A screwup. A recovering alcoholic. Unworthy of someone like her.

Looking through the cupboard again, he nearly chuckled when he found a bag of tiny marshmallows. Terry didn't seem like a hot chocolate kind of guy. The smile on his face didn't quite form as the thought rolled around. He probably kept it in here in remembrance of his little boy, not because he liked the hot drink.

Shaking off the negativity, he quickly heated up the milk in the microwave, added the cocoa mix to the cup, and dropped a few marshmallows on top of the steaming drink, and then headed toward Erin, who sat huddled in an afghan blanket close to the fire.

Trying to hold the drink steady, his hand failed him, shaking slightly when she grabbed it, her fingers grazing his.

"Thank you." A smile hid behind the cup as she took a small sip. "You didn't have to make this for me."

He shrugged as he took a seat on the floor near her, but not close enough to where he'd be tempted to pull her closer. Eventually, he'd have to hide out in the only room left, the bedroom. Because he didn't know how much self-control he had to stay away from her. Her rosy red cheeks, the way her silky brown hair looked mussed up from her hat. She looked so damn kissable right now, it was painful to stay away.

"I know you hate me, but—"

His gaze jerked to her. "I don't hate you."

That was the truth. She said she believed he didn't steal anything, and he believed her. Even before she told him that, he didn't hate her. He could never hate Erin. She didn't have a mean bone in her body. She always treated him with respect and like he was a normal person. Not like a man with so many problems it was hard to function on some days.

"You're..." Her eyes turned down to the shaggy brown carpet. "You don't seem happy to see me." Her eyes lifted, round like saucers. "Not that I expected you to be happy to see me. Of course not. That is not what I meant to say. Of course, it would be nice if you were, but, of course, you're not. That would be silly. Of course...I'm saying *of course* a lot. I'm going to stop talking." Her eyes drifted to the floor again.

A low chuckle slipped out. She was so damn adorable tongue-tied, he couldn't hold in the small laughter. He had never heard her so out of sorts before. Was he making her as nervous as he felt?

Her vibrant green eyes met his. He could stare into her eyes all night, get lost in the beauty of them, not regretting a moment.

"How's the hot chocolate? Can't say I've made it before." Damn it, that wasn't what he meant to say. He never had made it before, but he watched his sister do it. It hadn't looked too complicated.

"It's delicious. It's definitely warming me up. I swear I walked about a mile."

Another chuckle floated out. "Actually, I think it is about a mile." His brows puckered low, fear suddenly clutching his insides, twisting and turning until he thought he might throw up. "You could've gotten hurt, Erin."

"I needed to make sure you were okay. I can't explain it. I..." Worry, concern, and a hint of something else he couldn't quite decipher glittered in her green cat-like eyes. "I needed you to know you're not alone in this. I believe you."

Turning away, he stared into the blazing fire. He didn't

deserve her loyalty. He wasn't always a good man. He broke the law. Hurt his sister too many times to count. She shouldn't be so easily on his side without an explanation from him.

"James..." A tiny laugh drifted his way, filling his empty heart a fraction. "I'd say I'd leave you alone, but I'm kind of stuck here right now. I know you—"

"Stop." Whipping his attention back to her, he grabbed her loose hand on her lap. He had to reach for it, unable to stop himself when he heard the torture in her tone. He was tempted to scoot closer so he wasn't bent over awkwardly, but then he'd be even more tempted to wrap her in his arms and kiss her breathless.

Rubbing his thumb over her hand, his lips curled into a gentle smile. "Stop saying anything if it's something like I don't want you here. Because it's a lie. I am...I am happy you're here."

Whew! He couldn't believe he admitted that. His heart raced. His hand trembled. Could she feel it?

Biting her bottom lip, he could see a smile wanted to break free.

He let go of her hand before his impulsive control took over and he kissed her. "Finish your hot chocolate."

Raising the mug to her lips, she nodded. "Of course."

He couldn't tell with her sitting so close to the fire, but he swore her cheeks bloomed an even more rosy red as she repeated those same two words.

This was an adorable side of Erin he had never seen before. Tongue-tied and cute.

He loved it.

He loved...well, it wouldn't be hard to love Erin. But did he love her?

Standing up, he walked back to the kitchen before he

blurted out more things. Like maybe he did love her. She was an easy woman to love. And she would be a difficult woman to get over. He feared he might never get over her when he left town.

Because he was leaving no matter how much enticement sat before him.

6

ERIN WATCHED the flames dance before her, the fire finally warming her up from the long treacherous walk outside. She could hear James in the kitchen cleaning up the mess from the hot chocolate, not that she figured he made much of a mess.

He was uncomfortable. That's why he walked away after holding her hand briefly and saying he was happy she came.

She was happy, too. This was a chance to get to know him even more. Really talk to him, more than the idle chit chat when they were at work.

But she didn't know where to start.

Taking another sip of hot chocolate she thought he made to perfection, she tried to think of something easy and non-argumentative they could talk about. Something that wouldn't make her look like an idiot again.

And repeating *of course* so many times. What was the matter with her? Just like she repeated *okay* how many times with Theresa. She usually didn't get so tongue-tied and silly when it came to speaking, so she wasn't sure what the issue was tonight.

As she heard the water running in the kitchen, she rolled her eyes at her idiocy. Duh! She knew why she was acting all out of sorts.

She liked James.

She liked him a lot.

And she had no idea how to express that to him. Did he like her back? Would he want to pursue a relationship?

Mesmerized by the flames, her thoughts drifting in a million different directions, she jumped when James touched her shoulder. A bit of hot chocolate sloshed over the rim of her mug.

"I didn't mean to startle you. I said your name a few times, but you didn't answer." He gave her a crooked grin, crouching close to her.

Disappointment crushed her when his hand drifted away from her shoulder. But she couldn't let him see that. Whipping a smile out, she gave a half-hearted laugh. "Lost in thought. Sorry." Glancing down at the blanket, she grimaced. "I spilled hot chocolate on it. Sorry. I didn't mean to. I'm so clumsy sometimes. So sorry. If it doesn't come out, I'll replace it." Her eyes widened in horror. "I don't know how to knit. Was this knitted, or something else? I'm sorry. I—"

His hand touched her knee. "Erin...you're doing it again." A handsome smile punctured his lips. "It's adorable." He laughed. "And you have nothing to be sorry about. I didn't mean to startle you."

Thank goodness the fire was so close because she could feel her cheeks flaming a bright red. If he asked, she would blame it on the fire. Mumbling. Again. She had to stop it.

Not moving a muscle, almost like when a pet lay

comfortably on her lap and she didn't want to disturb them, she grinned. His hand still rested on her knee, and although it wasn't in a sexual, I-want-you kind of way, she liked it. She liked it a lot.

"You were calling my name..." She didn't know what else to say. *Please don't move your hand* sounded ridiculous. But that's what she wanted to say.

"I was just wondering..." His hand trembled but didn't move off her knee. "Umm...I was wondering if you were hungry."

She was definitely hungry. For so many things.

A kiss. A hug. A soft touch. For his hand to move a little higher. Oh, yes. She was very hungry.

"I'm okay."

Pressing her lips firmly together, she forced herself to stay silent. She would not repeat the word *okay* over and over again.

"Erin?" A pained expression touched his lips, then morphed into his eyes.

"Yes."

He looked at her, puzzled. Probably because she answered as a statement, an indicator he was free to do whatever he wanted—not as a question, wondering what he wanted to say. She wasn't completely positive what the tortured look that crossed over his face indicated, but if she had to take a guess...

He wanted to kiss her. Or was that wishful thinking again?

Abruptly, he snatched his hand away and stood up.

Apparently, it was her wishful thinking.

"I'll make you a sandwich."

But she wasn't hungry. She told him she was fine. Yet, he ran from her—again. She wasn't that well versed in flirting with guys or interpreting whether they liked her more than a friend, but she didn't think she was a complete idiot.

She swore she saw a hint of desire, even a strong need, in his eyes when he looked at her a minute ago.

Well, what was she going to do about it?

Sit here like a ninny and allow him to keep running away from the sexual tension that kept popping up between them? Because even at the hospital when he would stop to say hi, she swore a bit of sexual tension always swirled between them. She always chalked it up to her imagination. Because what would a sweet guy—although his life was filled with problems—an incredibly sweet guy, want with a girl like her? She had problems of her own. Not that she ever shared them with other people. The whole town didn't need to know everything, what her specific problems were. Sometimes things could be kept a secret.

Or she could get up and confront him. Ask him point-blank if he had feelings for her.

What a decision. A very serious, difficult decision.

Glancing toward the kitchen, she watched as he pulled out ingredients. His shoulders were straight and rigid, his movements smooth, yet with a slight tremble.

Decision made.

Unwrapping herself from the blanket, she stood up and set her hot chocolate on the mantel, then walked with determined steps to the kitchen.

He paused in slathering mayo on a piece of bread when she stopped right next to him. He quirked a brow high. "You don't like mayo?"

"I don't like when you walk away from me." She glanced at the bread, then back at his brown, almost piercing black eyes. "I don't mind mayo."

"I didn't walk away. I'm making you a sandwich."

"I didn't want a sandwich. I said I wasn't hungry."

He grinned as he tilted his head. "Actually, you said you were okay. You didn't necessarily say you weren't hungry. You might be hungry. That's why I'm making you a sandwich."

"Okay. I'm hungry."

A grin spread across his face. "I knew it."

"For you."

Silence descended. His jaw slacked. His mouth formed a small circle, his eyes round with shock. But silence surrounded them.

Well, she started this path, she had to finish it.

"Every time you've touched me tonight..." Oh, that was a bad way to start. She couldn't admit how his touch made her yearn for more. Or could she? She opened her mouth to finish, but nothing came out.

The shock had disappeared from his handsome face, his dark chocolate-colored eyes suddenly filled with pleasure. A brow rose. "Yes, please continue. My touch, what?"

She smiled, giggling. "I can't say it."

A low masculine chuckle returned her way as his lips curled into a tiny grin. "You didn't have a problem speaking earlier. Your new favorite word just a little bit ago was *sorry*, and before that, *of course*."

Slapping his shoulder playfully, she laughed as his grin grew into a smile. A rare smile that she wanted to keep seeing again and again. "Stop. Don't make fun of my ramblings." She bit her lip. "I like you, James. There. I said it."

His smile disappeared in a flash. "You shouldn't, Erin. I'm all kinds of wrong for you. If you weren't stuck here, I'd ask you to leave. You don't belong here. You don't belong with the likes of me."

Her heart broke for each word laced with anguish. A deep, wrenching anguish where he honestly thought he wasn't worth her time.

Damn the town for making him feel like an outsider.

"Your touch makes me crave more. So if you're not going to give it to me, I'll just take it myself." Then she stepped forward, framed his face with her hands, loving the feel of his soft beard, and pressed her lips to his.

HE STOOD STOCK-STILL, shock coating his veins, making him freeze like a gnome statue sitting in a pretty garden. He had never had a woman be so brazen and confident with him. Sure, he had his fair share of women, mostly just for sex. Dating never entered into the equation. It was always about sex.

The knife fell from his hand, clattering to the counter.

This...

Erin in his arms...

This was *not* about sex.

His arms slid around her waist, pulling her closer as he took control of the kiss, deepening it, forcing her to open her mouth. She didn't resist, tangling tongues with him immediately. Her hands slid across his cheeks and through his hair, where they rested against the back of his neck, sending tingling bolts of desire straight through him.

It spurred him into further action—something he shouldn't do. This desire. This want. This intense need for her, something he felt the first time he met her. He should ignore it all. Except he didn't. Turning her slightly, he held her captive against the counter, pressing into her, showing her how much he wanted her.

A low, sexy moan escaped her lips as her fingers tugged on the back of his hair. The kiss turned hotter. So hot, like sitting on top of a fire. Tongues clashed, hands roamed, murmurs and low moans echoed around the kitchen.

He wanted to strip her naked and make love to her right next to the fireplace. He wanted to see the soft glow touch her skin, haloing her like the angel she was.

No.

He couldn't.

He was leaving. Never coming back. Never returning to this dumb town with all its dumb inhabitants.

Hands tightening on her waist, maybe too tight when he heard a small squeak between their lips, he pulled away.

"We can't do this."

Her fingers brushed the back of his neck, increasing the desire begging to be released.

"We're two healthy adults, alone in a cabin. I think we can do anything we want."

It wouldn't take much to convince him. His resolve was near nonexistent.

"I don't have any condoms."

It was the only thing that popped into his head that would stop the madness before him. And it was. Complete and utter madness. He couldn't continue to touch, explore, devour this gorgeous woman more than he already had. Because the second he left, a part of his heart and soul would stay attached to Erin.

Who was he kidding? A part of it already had attached to her the minute his lips touched hers. She tasted so good and sweet, so full of everything he'd never be.

When she said nothing, and just stared at him while her fingers massaged the back of his neck, his brows dipped low into a frown. "I said I don't have any condoms."

A sweet angelic smile sprang upon her lips. "I heard you. I'm trying to think back when I last took my birth control pills." Her smile faltered. "I think it's been three days. I'm terrible at remembering to take it consistently."

His self-control was wavering, even with the knowledge she missed a few pills, the likelihood of getting pregnant a possibility. He wanted to slam his lips upon hers. He wanted to slide deep inside and show her how much he loved her.

Damn.

He did love her.

But he was leaving.

With more strength than he thought possible, he pushed away from her, dropping his hands from her waist. Her hands fell to her sides when he moved far enough away from her that she couldn't hold onto him. She couldn't brush her delicate fingers against his neck, something he enjoyed. He missed her touch immediately.

"So, that's that, uh?" A sad smile twisted her lips. "We could always try this another time. When we do have condoms around."

"I'm the wrong person for you, Erin."

She threw her hands up in the air, clearly exasperated. "Why, James? Why are you such a terrible person?"

Holding up his hand, he started to tick off reason after reason for her, starting with his pointer finger. "I'm a shitty brother. I used to steal from Theresa when I had no money, and I needed a drink so badly I didn't care how much I hurt her." The second finger went up. "I'm an alcoholic. Every day I want a drink. I am almost two years sober, but it's still a struggle." The third finger went up. "I have a record. I've done some terrible shit in my life. I even hit Aiden...and I don't regret it." His fourth finger snapped up. "I have such horrible judgment with people, I was friends with an asshole that tried to kill my sister by setting her house on fire." The last and final finger went up. "I barely graduated high school and I never went to college. I'm a loser, Erin. I have no experience in anything. Working at the hospital was the longest job I've ever had and I couldn't even manage to keep that one."

She stared at him, a little wide-eyed, but not much else was written in her expression. He couldn't quite decipher what she was thinking.

No response to his outburst either.

Inhaling and exhaling, he tried to relax his stance as he lowered his hand. "I'm leaving, Erin. This town has never wanted me, and I sure as hell don't want it anymore. I didn't steal any drugs. Thank you for believing in me when so few do."

With that, he walked out of the kitchen and straight to the bathroom, locking the door behind him. Grasping the sides of the sink, he squeezed hard, dying to release an anguished scream. He kept it to himself as he stared hard at the person back in the mirror.

Well, now she knew what kind of guy he was. Although, she'd probably heard it all before.

In case she hadn't, now she knew.

He was a loser, and he would never be good enough for her.

7

THE SILENCE in the kitchen grated on her nerves as she stood frozen in the same spot since James walked away. She would've preferred he stayed, talking and letting it all out. The silence was a little too much to bear.

It was as if she were back outside, the cold filling her up, turning her into an icicle. She wanted to move, go find him, say something. But she couldn't find the strength.

She knew everything about him that he shouted at her, thanks to living in a small town. Although she wasn't positive he knew he was yelling when he ticked off each item methodically on his fingers. He had been in a zone, cut off from everything but what was circling his mind.

It didn't change how she felt about him. Everyone made mistakes. Nobody was perfect. And anybody in town who thought they were better than him was lying to themselves. He was a good person. He helped people around the hospital, giving directions, lending a hand when they needed assistance. Yet, his job was to mop the floors and empty the trash. She even saw him buy someone a cold pop when he was running on fumes waiting for news on his wife, who was having a complicated birth. His nerves and anxiety had been so ramped up, he couldn't even be in the room with her. James saw him pacing the emergency room, the farthest place away from his wife. The man didn't touch the pop, but he had stopped his pacing to converse with James. The man started to relax as they talked about random things. Then James walked out of the area with the guy next to him.

Yes, he made mistakes. But that didn't make him unworthy of love.

A shiver raced up her spine.

The word didn't sound foreign in her mind.

Love.

For almost a year, she anticipated, ached for James to arrive to work so he'd come visit her at her desk. No, it wasn't so far off the spectrum to think she loved him. She might've gotten to know him unconventionally, talking with him, yet not in a date-like setting, but she still got to know him. The real him. She didn't think a moment they spent together was fake.

She made mistakes in her life, too. She was far from perfect.

Rotating her shoulders, brushing her fingers across her lips, remembering his warm lips devouring hers, she went in search of him. It wasn't too difficult to find he was hiding in the bathroom. Standing in front of the door, a smile twisted her lips. Was he going to stay in there all night long?

Knocking on the door, she decided even if he wanted to, she wasn't going to let him. "Can I come in?" She rolled her eyes. The bathroom wasn't the place for this kind of conversation. "Or can you come out?"

"Go away, Erin. I'm taking a shit."

Laughter broke free. "You're a damn liar, James. You are not. Stop running from me. Stop walking away when we're having a conversation. We all have pasts. Some we might even regret. It doesn't make you a bad person…or a loser."

Her hands fisted as she remembered the way he uttered that one word.

Loser.

I'm a loser, Erin.

The conviction in his tone. The miserable way he said it. He truly believed it.

He would not shut her out. She wouldn't allow it. Maybe he thought she was a calm, sweet woman who stood back when things happened. Because, yes, at work, she tended to let others handle the difficult stuff. Unless it was her job, manning the front desk, to step in and restore order.

She could be calm and sweet.

She could also be in-your-face and determined.

He was about to find that out.

Twisting the knob, it jerked in her hand. The handle rattled as she shook it harder. "Unlock the door, James. This is ridiculous."

He locked her out. It was…childish.

And yet, the only defense mechanism at his disposal right now.

Leaning her forehead against the door, she held her hand up in front of her, holding her pointer finger out first. "I never finished college. Although I was very close. I work the front desk at the hospital, not because I love it, but because I never finished college and I'm not a nurse. I can't be a nurse." A tremble shook her. "I'm okay with that. Not finishing college was a blessing. I realized I didn't want to be a nurse. I'm happy behind that desk. People think I finished college, though. I just don't correct them when they say it."

She paused, waiting for him to say something. Nothing but silence answered. She held up another finger. "I haven't seen my sister in over five years. I haven't even talked to her. When I told her I was moving to help our aunt and uncle, she laughed in my face and said they weren't worth it." She sucked in a sharp breath. "I told her she wasn't worth it. I didn't mean it, but I still said it." Her third finger went up before she lost the courage to finish. "I don't regret coming to help, but I see my sister's side of the argument. My uncle is a difficult man. I want to hate him. And I don't like hating people. It sounds so harsh."

Freezing, stalling more words, she listened as she heard a noise on the other side of the door. She couldn't make out what he was doing, but he wasn't speaking so she decided to forge on. Her fourth finger went up. "Remember that big mess, all that water on the floor in the emergency room about a month ago? Well, I might've poured it on the floor on purpose." She stopped when she thought she heard him curse. "I was having a bad day, although hiding it well, and I wanted to see you, talk to you. I had to use the only excuse I could come up with. A mess for you to clean up." A strangled laugh released as her fifth finger popped up. This would be a hard one to admit. "Long before I even met you, I...I had a crush on Aiden."

She had no time to prepare when the door swung open, losing her balance since she had been resting her forehead against the door. Luckily for her, she landed in his arms. One of his hands caught her around the waist and hung on tightly as she pressed her hands against his hard, warm chest.

His eyes sparkled with rage. "But that crush is over, right? He's married to my sister."

A tiny corner of her lip inched up. "That's been long over. If I would've known you were going to whip open the door so fast like that, I would've started with that one."

She could tell he didn't want to, but a smile started to form on his handsome, angered face.

Reaching up, she brushed a hand across his roughened jaw—loving the fact that she could touch his beard and soak up the wonderment—then swept it up through his hair and to the back of his neck. She swore she heard him sigh with contentment. "We all have pasts, James. They aren't pretty. None of them are."

His lips curved into a wider smile. "You really created a mess so I'd help you?"

Biting her lip, she couldn't hide her smile. "I really did. Do you hate me for it?"

His mouth came down, caressing her lips lightly. "You can make any mess you like and I'll always clean it up." He lifted his other hand loose by their sides with a box securely in his grip. "I found a box of condoms underneath the sink."

"Well, that was lucky."

The smile on his face died, although the passion and need flaming in his intense gaze never faltered. "I can't promise you anything, Erin. I'm leaving town. I'm not changing my mind. But it doesn't change the fact that I want you. I want you right now."

Her heart ached, a tiny pinprick of pain every time he said he was leaving.

But she couldn't worry about it. She only wanted one thing.

Him.

"I want you, too."

A tender smile graced his lips right before they captured hers.

SHE TASTED sweet like chocolate and felt warm and soft in his arms. The box of condoms clutched in his hand had been a blessing when he found it digging underneath the sink. A real blessing. Because he would've stayed locked inside the bathroom all night long if he hadn't found them.

That's how much he wanted Erin in his arms.

And now she was.

Drifting away from her lips, he smiled, remembering the way she said she made a water mess just to get his attention. He never knew she liked him. It filled him up with a little bit of hope. Something he hadn't felt in the longest time. Maybe ever.

"You're smiling at me. Why?" The delicate grin gracing her lips made him ache to claim her mouth again. And again. And again.

"Because I can." He didn't know what else to say. His mind was a jumble of emotions, and focusing was a weakness at the moment. Except focusing on making her feel good, tasting her from head to toe, he wouldn't call that a weakness at all.

"Are we planning on standing here all night or..."

A cocky brow arched as his smile spread. "Or. Definitely or."

She giggled as he lowered his mouth near her neck and smothered her with kisses. Wrapping his arms around her, he picked her up, making her swing her legs around his waist, then started walking toward the fireplace. He could've headed for the bedroom, but he wanted to see her in front of the fire, the beautiful glow lighting up her skin, haloing her beauty.

When he set her down on the couch, the smile spread across her face said she wanted the same thing. To make love in front of the fire.

He tossed the box of condoms on the floor near the fireplace, then grabbed a thick blanket from the chest against the wall and laid it down in front of the fire. He also grabbed two pillows from the bedroom. Maybe they'd even sleep out here tonight. He wasn't sure, but while they were on the floor, he wanted her to be as comfortable as possible.

As he walked out of the bedroom with two pillows, one in each hand, he stopped in his tracks, short of reaching his destination. Erin lay on the floor on top of the cream-colored blanket dressed in only her bra and white lace panties.

The gentle light from the flames lit up each part of her body in an elegant glow, just like he imagined. Haloed before him like an angel.

"You're gaping, James. Come here." She patted the floor next to her.

How could he not gape? She was pure perfection, and she was about to taint herself with him.

Before that disastrous thought could take hold and ruin the moment, she smiled, sliding a hand down her chest, across her stomach, stopping short of touching the waistband of her panties.

"Am I taking these off, or are you?"

It spurred him into action. He wouldn't—couldn't—let his melancholy mood ruin the night. Because that's all he'd get with her.

One night.

One glorious night.

He planned to enjoy every second of it.

Tossing the pillows to the floor, near her head but not on top of it, he chuckled when she laughed.

"We can have a pillow fight later. Get naked. Now." The

need in her eyes was so intense, his knees almost buckled. He wasn't about to refuse her anything.

He shed his clothes, every last piece, then joined her on the floor.

Gliding a hand down her cheek in slow increments, he made his way down her neck to her breasts, circling one nipple with his finger, then the other. Then he kept gliding his hand down her stomach where he stopped at the same place she did.

"You are pure perfection, Erin. Every beautiful, soft inch of you." He pressed a kiss to her cheek.

Her hand reached over and caressed his jaw. "You're pretty damn magnificent yourself. I didn't know you were so toned."

He knew what he looked like because he stared at himself in the mirror too many times to count. Staring, wondering, judging himself. It was a battle he had yet to win. Some days, he wanted to break the mirror—he hated what looked back at him. He wouldn't necessarily call himself toned. Yeah, he worked out, but he didn't have a six-pack or anything crazy.

He wasn't toned. He wasn't anything pretty to look at.

Her hand trailed from his face and down his arm where she squeezed his bicep. "Definitely toned. Start believing the compliments I give you. Does no one ever compliment you?"

His brows puckered low into a frown. Did he say that last thing out loud? In a whisper, maybe? He must've by the sad look in her eyes and her soft words that filled up a part of his broken soul.

"Besides my sister, nobody cares about me, Erin." He looked away toward the flames dancing before them. "Some days, I can't figure out why she cares either. I hurt her."

"Well, now you have two people who care about you. You're trying, James. That's why she cares." Her hand pressed against his cheek again, forcing him to look at her. "You have a beautiful soul. You just don't see it as I do." Her eyes glittered with sudden bliss. "Now, are you going to remove my panties and bra and make sweet love to me or not?"

Oh, he was going to make sweet, sweet love to her.

All night long.

And treasure this night for the rest of his life.

His hand grasped the side of her panties and slid them down her legs. Next, he tackled her bra with ease, teasing and nibbling her nipples as he did. He tossed the bra behind him, not even paying attention to where it landed. Clamping his mouth around a hard, taut nipple, he suckled, nipped, and lavished her with the pleasure of his lips as his fingers dove into her soft, warm heat below.

He teased and tortured her with his mouth and fingers until her low moans filling the room turned into a delightful cry of ecstasy. A lot quicker than he anticipated. Tilting his gaze to hers, he waited for her to open her eyes.

Brushing a hand up her delicate body, he cradled her cheek and met her lips with his. "You're so responsive. So damn beautiful."

A shy, awkward smile touched her lips. "It's been a while." She closed her eyes since she couldn't move her head away with his hand holding her cheek. "It's been a very long while."

"Look at me, Erin."

Her eyes popped open.

"I love how responsive you are. How many times do you think I can make you orgasm tonight?"

A sweet, yet seductive smile twisted her lips. "Oh, I don't know. But I'm willing to find out."

He kissed her hard across the lips, digging his tongue, twirling and tangoing with her as if they were dancing, bodies draped close to each other. His one hand still held her cheek while his other hand reached out to find the box of condoms. He never once let go of her wonderful lips as he found his objective and grabbed a package.

Moving slowly, he went from lying by her side to on top of her. The package crinkled as he opened it, his mouth still devouring her, showing her how much he desired her. She returned every powerful twist of his lips with a twist of her own, her hands wrapped tightly around his neck, her fingers digging in his hair just the way he loved.

The condom went on quickly, then he positioned himself. Without breaking the intense kiss setting his body on fire, he slid into her with ease. So wet and hot for him. She fit him perfectly.

Her fingers dug into his hair, pulling, yanking, as he started to move in and out.

She met him thrust for thrust just as perfectly as she met him kiss for kiss.

In and out.

Over and over.

The heat from the fire touching his skin wasn't even close to the heat touching his body from her breathtaking touch.

He broke the kiss, sending a trail of kisses across her cheek to her neck and ended at her ear.

"Pure perfection, Erin. So. Damn. Perfect." He enunciated each word as he pounded into her a little harder.

She met each thrust with eager enthusiasm, clutching, grabbing, and stroking the back of his neck and hair.

"Harder, James. I want more. I need more," she whispered into his ear with short, heavy breaths. Then she bit his shoulder.

The pain hit immediately, as did the bliss from her teeth grazing his skin. He couldn't be sure, but he swore she left a mark on his skin.

Branded him.

Oh, yes. He would brand her, too.

His thrusts became harder, more intense as she requested.

Low groans and grunts slipped from his lips in between the kisses he showered upon her neck and ear. He even lightly bit her shoulder in return. A sweet, delicate moan echoed in response as her hands tightened around his neck.

Like an avalanche of snow heading straight for them, they erupted together, tensed, frozen in place as a deep pleasure spread throughout.

He paused, enjoying the tingling sensation coating his veins as her fingers brushed the back of his neck and a little down his back.

He had to be crushing her, though. He started to move, but her grip around him tightened, stalling his movement.

"Don't move."

A kiss touched her neck, then to the spot he bit her, a few teeth marks glaring at him. Damn. He bit her harder than he thought. He pressed a few more kisses in the same place, hoping to soothe the pain he must've inflicted.

"I hurt you." He stiffened. A powerful ache swept through him. That was the last thing he ever wanted to do. The bliss from moments before disappeared instantly.

It didn't matter how hard he tried, he always hurt the people he cared about.

8

AIDEN RUBBED his hands as the heat from the vents in his patrol vehicle blasted on high. He glanced to his right when his passenger side door opened. Bentley slid in and quickly shut the door.

"How's it going? Crazy storm, huh?"

Bentley nodded, shivering and rubbing his gloved hands together. "Yeah. We've helped so many people out of the ditch tonight, it's beyond crazy. Thanks for helping with this latest one. How long are you working tonight?"

He had no clue, but he hoped he'd be done soon. When he was out in weather like this, Theresa worried, and he didn't need her worrying even more than she already was. This shit with her brother had amped up her anxiety. Add in the issues with—

Well, thinking about it right now wasn't the time or place.

"As long as Chief Duncan needs me. How about you? How's Emma?"

"I'm on for another two hours and then switching with Charlie." Bentley trembled in his seat, rubbing his hands harder. "Emma's good. She was snuggled under the thick blanket my mom made for her birthday and a cup of hot chocolate when I left. She was complaining she couldn't add any alcohol to it." Bentley chuckled. "I thought she was a firecracker before she got pregnant. Now that she's four months along, her hormones are off the charts. Sometimes it's like walking in a minefield when I talk to her."

Aiden laughed along, even though he knew Bentley didn't find it that funny. His best friend honestly worried he'd say or do the wrong thing a little too much. But Aiden didn't think he had anything to worry about. Bentley put a ring on her finger six months ago, and four months ago they got the news they were expecting. Bentley had nothing to worry about. She wasn't leaving. She was here for the long haul, even if they hadn't set a wedding date yet.

He was happy for his friend. He truly was. Except it hurt—

Nope. Not the time or place to let those thoughts in.

Time to focus on something new.

"Did you hear about James?"

Bentley nodded as concern flickered in his gaze. "I'm pretty damn sure the whole town heard. A blizzard doesn't stop the gossip. How's Theresa?"

"Taking it hard. James stopped by. He didn't look like he was in a good place." Aiden sighed, running a hand down his face. "He annoys me more often than not, but he's her brother. So he's my family, too. I stick by my family. I called Chief Duncan."

"About what? Is the hospital pressing charges? Are they expecting you to arrest him or something?"

"That's the thing. They aren't pressing charges." Aiden shook his head, his eyes filled with disbelief. "Don't you find that odd? A bunch of prescription drugs go missing and all you do is fire the guy for stealing them, not press charges."

Bentley frowned. "So...you want them to press charges?"

"Hell, no. I want them to tell the truth. I don't think James stole anything. They're using him as a scapegoat or something."

"What did Chief Duncan say?"

Aiden gazed out the window at the wind blowing, the snow swirling around in a frenzy. "He said as soon as this storm blows over, he'll get to the bottom of it." He turned toward Bentley. "Don't know what that entails, but if he says he'll take care of it, I believe him. James doesn't deserve what happened to him."

"He's lucky to have you on his side."

A chuckle let loose. "Can you remind him of that? He still hates me most of the time. And I don't know why. I treat Theresa right. I even try to be nice to him."

Bentley waved a hand as if indicating he should blow it off. "It's all from our high school days. He always hated us jocks. That's probably how he still sees us. Let me know if you need anything. Emma and I will be there right away."

"Thanks, man. I appreciate it."

"So..."

Aiden's brows lowered in confusion at Bentley's sudden hesitation. "Yeah?"

Bentley cleared his throat, averting his eyes. "It might not be the time or place to say..."

"Okay? I have no clue what you're trying to say."

Bentley looked him straight in the eye. "I told you Emma's hormones have been off the charts, right? I don't know. Maybe she has a six sense or something. I don't know. She thinks...I don't know...she..."

Aiden slapped him on the shoulder, laughing. "Just spit it out, dude."

"Are you and Theresa trying to get pregnant?"

His laughter died immediately, his attention snapping to the snow blowing like a dust storm outside, unable to look his best friend in the eye. Bentley was right. This wasn't the time or place. Especially when he'd been trying his damnedest not to think about it when he was alone in his car, driving around, responding to accident calls.

"Shit. She is right. I'm sorry for bringing it up."

With the hurt and pain in Bentley's tone, he jerked his gaze back to him. "We've been trying for almost a year. It's been stressing Theresa out, which might not help the situation. And now this shit with her brother, that doesn't help her stress. We're happy for you and Emma, Bentley. Don't think we're not."

"I know." Bentley frowned, his gaze lowering, then snapping back up. "Don't forget I'm here for you. You kept that shit about Cynthia to yourself for a long time and I hated it. I'm always here for you."

Aiden slapped him on the shoulder again, this time leaving his hand there and squeezing. Talking about Cynthia—a woman he was once engaged to before she died in a car accident—was never a conversation he wanted to have, but Bentley was right. "I know. It's not something we like to talk about with other people. Not until we know what we're doing."

"Like treatment or something?"

"Yeah. We've talked about seeing a specialized doctor that can give us some guidance. We haven't decided yet. Maybe after the holidays. Definitely something we'll talk about after we help out James."

Bentley shook his head as a soft chuckle floated out. "He has no idea how lucky he is to have you guys in his life. I hope he gets that stick out of his ass soon."

Aiden chuckled with him. "You're starting to sound like Emma."

Bentley beamed a bright smile. "She does rub off on me."

He looked away, glancing out the window for the umpteenth time, thinking of Theresa, her brother James, and all the problems they'd been facing lately. He'd been through so much in his life, he knew they could tackle these hurdles, too.

First, James.

Then, baby issues. Again, not something he wanted to think about right now.

"Looks like your crew's gearing up to leave. Stay safe out there."

Bentley nodded, rubbed his hands together one more time, then opened his door. "Stay safe as well. Keep me updated about...everything."

"I promise I will."

Some things wouldn't be easy to talk about, but he wouldn't lie to his friend anymore. Not like he did for too many years.

Watching the snow fall, he wished it'd stop already so he could solve problem number one. The issue with James.

He wondered how he was faring, all alone in the cabin in the woods. Maybe being alone wasn't the best thing for him.

Well, at least he had no alcohol near him out there.

SHE RELAXED IN THE LOWLIGHT, the heat from the fire warming her up, but the chills attacked her body. James ran again. He tensed in her arms, then abruptly disengaged from her and all but ran to the bathroom, where he shut the door with a loud click.

He had kissed her in the same spot he bit her, then uttered with a pained tone, "I hurt you."

Foolish man. He didn't hurt her. Sure, there was a mark, which would account for his behavior, but he hadn't hurt her when he bit down. It felt euphoric. Wonderful. Intense pleasure.

Before he walked away, she had seen the love bite— that's what she'd call it—on his shoulder. So if he wanted to say he hurt her, then she hurt him, too.

She didn't know what to do. Did she keep attacking his emotions, getting in his face? Or was she driving him away every time she refused to let him run away from her?

Well, she wasn't a quitter. Chuckling out loud, she shook her head. Most of the time she wasn't a quitter. She didn't finish school. That said quitter loud and clear.

But when it became rough, so tough it was hard to hold her tongue and say nothing, she was no quitter.

Because some of the things her uncle said sometimes, it was so difficult not to just up and leave and say *screw you*.

Slowly sitting up, she decided she'd give James a few more minutes and then she would bang on the door.

Turning to the flames dancing merrily before her, a sadness pierced her heart. For James. For her aunt. For herself.

And that was the last thing she should be feeling after the most amazing sex she had. His soft touch. His hard thrusts. The way they moved together. She never felt anything like that before. She wanted to feel it again. And again. And again.

But she believed him when he said he was leaving. She wouldn't be winning that battle.

Did she even have a chance to win the war? Capture his heart and lay victory to his love?

A scream tore from her lips and she jumped when a hand landed on her shoulder. She started laughing, matching the sweet grin on James' face.

Pressing a hand to her mouth to hold back the laughter she couldn't seem to control, she stared into his chocolate brown eyes that held a bit of pain and regret.

"I didn't mean to startle you." His hand slid down her arm and then fell to his side as he was kneeled beside her. "You look like such an angel, all your beauty haloed by the firelight. It takes my breath away, Erin." His hand reached out, barely brushing the mark on her shoulder, yet the touch felt like a bolt of lightning straight to her heart. "So when I hurt you..." A harsh groan left his mouth. "It guts me."

His hand still hovered near her shoulder, wanting to touch, yet not. She grabbed his hand, pushing it toward his shoulder where she could see the love bite she left him. "I hurt you, too."

"I know. I saw." His eyes were turned away from her, watching the fire blaze before them.

"So why is it terrible you think you hurt me, but it doesn't matter I hurt you?"

His eyes jerked to hers. "There's no thinking about it, Erin. I *did* hurt you."

She took his hand from his shoulder and guided it to her breast. "You made me feel the most pleasure I've ever experienced. Why don't you do it again? And again. And again until I can't move from this spot."

His eyes dilated with bliss at her bold words.

"You can bite me as much as you want." She leaned closer and pressed her lips to his neck, nibbling before sinking her teeth in.

A low sound, something between a groan and growl, fell from his lips. His hand took control, squeezing her breast, tweaking her nipple, eliciting her own soft moan.

"It's not hurting me when you show me how much you care. You do care about me, right, James? Tell me this isn't just sex. I don't want it to be just that."

Her heart started to pound as she placed small kisses along his neck. She couldn't believe she confessed her real feelings. Actually pleaded with him to give her the truth.

Hearing the truth wasn't always the best thing. But right here, in this moment, she needed the truth.

He was leaving, yes, she understood that. But she needed to know he wasn't using her for sex. She wanted this to mean something. To both of them.

His hand dropped from her breast, his posture tense.

She tensed as well, hating what was about to come out of his mouth.

His hands gripped her shoulders and pushed her away as his deep brown gaze filled with such anguish connected with hers.

"I can't define what this is, Erin. But I can say it's not just sex." His expression fell into such intense pain she wanted to reach out and embrace him hard. Let him know she would always be there for him. "I can't give you what you want. I don't know how." His fingers tightened around her shoulders, pulling her closer, his lips precariously close to hers. "But it will never be just sex between us. It's some-thing...more."

His lips melted upon hers. Slow, sweet, and sensual. Telling her with each small movement his words held no lies.

The kiss ended too soon. James leaned away, sitting down next to her. His hands were on his lap, yet she could see it in his features, in the way his entire body still looked tense and ready to spring to action, that he wanted to touch her. She wouldn't stop him. She didn't know why he let go of her to begin with.

She was losing him. Not that she ever had him. Body, yes. Soul, not even close. And that's what she wanted. His body and soul. His...love.

Looking away toward the flames, a heavy sigh released. She knew every sordid thing about him, thanks to living in a small town and gossip running freely and easily. But he didn't know much about her. He didn't know the pains she had to deal with.

"My aunt has Alzheimer's." He looked her way when that's all she said. "I moved here to help my uncle. At the time I moved, it wasn't as progressive as it is now. My sister said I shouldn't come. Not to slight our aunt or anything, but because she didn't want me around my uncle. I'm not sure what kind of falling out my dad and my uncle had, but we didn't see my aunt and uncle very often."

He grabbed her hand, squeezing, as if telling her it was all going to be okay and that she could either continue or not. It was up to her. She felt all of that in one simple squeeze.

"My dad didn't even tell me I shouldn't go. He just said, 'It's your choice.' So I was confused by my sister's insistence

I not go. I get it now. After five years of dealing with that asshole, I get it."

His grip turned fierce. "Did he hurt you?"

Her eyes held his gaze, even when she wanted to look away. "Sometimes, yes. In a way. I don't know how I managed to keep that kind of secret from the town. Or how he continues to get away with it."

His jaw clenched, his dark mocha-colored eyes blazing with rage. "Some things don't always get known around here. You're pretty good about keeping things about you close to your chest. But I want to know how he hurt you."

She wanted to smile to erase the intensity on his face, but she couldn't manage to produce one. "He never laid a hand on me, if that's what you're wondering."

"You don't always need to touch someone to hurt them, Erin. I should know. I hurt Theresa a lot by stealing from her and saying shit I shouldn't have."

She turned her eyes to the floor. "He's good at emotionally tearing you apart. Little jabs here. Little jabs there." Her gaze shot to his. "I only held my tongue and stayed this long for my aunt. I'm almost happy she has Alzheimer's," her voice cracked, "and that's such a terrible thing to say. But he can't hurt her as badly if she doesn't remember. And yet, he is hurting her."

His expression hardened into a look that frightened her. Not for herself, either. But for her uncle. "I won't let him hurt you ever again."

She leaned his way, kissing him softly in thanks. "I don't see him often. My aunt's gotten so bad, he finally had to hire an in-home nurse. I tried to talk him into sending her to a facility where she could get the best care, but he won't relinquish that control. And he's all about the control."

"So why do you stay if you're not helping anymore?"

Scooting closer, wrapping her arms around his waist, resting her head against his chest, she exhaled in contentment when his arms circled her, cocooning her with his safety and comfort.

"Because I met you. I looked forward to our little chats." She pressed harder into his embrace. "Because I wasn't ready to let you go."

9

JAMES FLIPPED THE EGGS, then glanced over to where Erin lay sleeping in front of the fire. His lips widened into a smile he wasn't used to displaying very often. But thinking about her, her beautiful body, the sweet sounds she made while making love over and over again last night, kept making him smile.

They never even made it to the bedroom. They spent all night in front of the fire, kissing, caressing, and talking. One thing after another until they fell asleep.

When sunlight started to pour through the window, it woke him up. For a while, he laid there with her, brushing her hair with a light hand, reveling in the beauty in his arms.

Never in his wildest dreams did he ever think he'd have Erin in his arms. Never.

But last night he did. All night long.

The things they talked about...

He shoved the button down on the toaster hard as he thought about her uncle, the things she said about him. The things he would say to her, the way he would tear her down, treat her like she was an imbecile, incompetent.

She was everything wonderful in this world. Sweet, kind, compassionate. She didn't deserve anyone saying anything bad about her.

And if he stuck around, dating her, the town would also have plenty to say to—and about—her.

Which she didn't seem to mind. She hadn't once said or asked him to stay. She accepted it for what it was. Something he wanted. Needed.

Three more days until Christmas. He promised Theresa he'd come over for Christmas dinner and he decided he couldn't break his promise.

Glancing at Erin, he wondered if he could talk her into staying a few more days with him, tucked away from the world in this tiny little cabin.

He could show her how much he loved her without saying the actual words and live off the beautiful memories when he left town.

The toast popped up. Grabbing the butter out of the fridge, he slathered it over the two pieces of toast, then pulled the bacon out of the oven and slid the eggs onto a plate. Retrieving a tray from a bottom cupboard, he loaded it up and brought the breakfast to Erin, setting it gently on the floor near their makeshift bed.

Kissing her lightly on the lips, he woke her up, running his hand down her side, cupping her hip.

"Mmm...something smells good," she whispered against his lips, her eyes still closed.

"I made you breakfast, sw—" He cut the last word off before he made a colossal fool of himself.

He couldn't call her sweetheart. She wasn't his sweetheart. She wasn't his anything, no matter how much he ached for her to be something in his life.

Something permanent.

Something more than just friends sleeping together.

Her eyes opened, pressing her lips against his one more time. "Breakfast in bed." Glancing at the fire, she giggled. "Well, sort of. You're so sweet. I've never had breakfast in bed before."

Good.

That was a very good thing.

Maybe it wouldn't be too hard to persuade her to spend the next few days in the cabin with him.

"It's nothing fancy, so don't get too excited," he said with a chuckle, then kissed her one more time as he squeezed her hip.

Then he backed away and placed the tray on her lap after she sat up. Grabbing one of the plates for himself, they both dug in.

"So—"

"I was—"

Laughter filled the tiny cabin. He decided he'd let her go first because he still didn't know how to get the words out about her staying with him.

Waving his hand for her to continue, he smiled and took a bite of his eggs.

She nodded, biting her bottom lip as she fiddled with her fork, glancing around the room. "So..."

He locked in on her nervous gaze, the adorable way she bit her lip. He'd never get tired of looking at the beauty before him. "The suspense is killing me, Erin." He laughed. So did she.

Her sweet laughter filled up a part of his damaged soul he never thought would heal.

"So, my car is stuck." She scraped her fork around her plate. "Your car is stuck."

"Yep."

She bit her lip again. "It's still snowing out."

He looked out the window, surprised to see it snowing. When he woke up to prepare breakfast, not a drop of snow fell to the ground.

"It is."

"Right, it is. So..." Her eyes rounded as hysterical laughter left her charming lips. "Oh my gosh. I'm doing it again. I keep saying *so* too much."

"Whatever it is, you can tell me, Erin. I can dig you out and get your car back on the road." He looked down at his plate, unable to look her in the eyes any longer. "You probably need to get to work."

A soft, gentle hand touched his cheek. He raised his gaze to her shimmering green eyes, the desire sparkling like the beautiful glow of lights on a Christmas tree.

"So I guess...if you don't mind..." Her hand trembled against his cheek. "How about I stay another day. Since we're kind of snowed in."

"You want to stay? With me?"

She moved closer, pressing her lips to his. "So badly."

His hand reached for her waist, pulling her a bit closer, yet making sure the plate on his lap didn't fall. "I'm starting to like this word *so* you keep using."

She giggled, then kissed him again. "So we agree? You don't mind if I stick around?"

"Hell, no. I want you to stay." He sighed, his hand tensing and tightening on her waist. "What about work?"

"I'm off until the twenty-seventh." Her hand caressed his cheek, then fell to her side. "But, honestly, after the way they treated you, they can go screw themselves."

"I don't want you to get fired because of me, Erin."

She shrugged. "Okay. I'll quit then."

He leaned away, setting his plate on the tray she had moved from her lap when she scooted closer to him.

"You can't do that."

"Why not?"

"Because I'm—"

She pressed a finger to his lips. "If you're about to put yourself down and say something like you're not worth it, I'm going to..." Her lips curled into a seductive smile. "Bite you."

His mouth opened and her finger fell inside. He closed his mouth, sucking on her finger as she pulled it away from him in a slow, teasing manner. "You're threatening to bite me?"

"That's right."

His body tightened in response, the heat, the pleasure swarming his veins. Damn, but he wanted her to bite him again.

But he also didn't want her quitting her job because of him. He wasn't worth it, no matter what she said.

He didn't want to talk about this right now. Not ever, if he had his way.

The conversation was over.

He stood up and looked out the window.

Then he looked at her.

"What do you think about building a snowman?"

HE WAS RUNNING AWAY from his issues again. But Erin needed to pick and choose her battles carefully. She didn't have hope she'd win the war, but that didn't mean she was going to give up easily.

She stood up, meeting his playful grin she knew he had to force out.

"I'd love to build a snowman."

Thankfully, right before her eyes, his grin turned into a real one as the pleasure lit his gaze. "Let's finish breakfast and go play in the snow."

He grabbed the tray from the floor and they finished their meal in the kitchen with minimal conversation, which was for the best. She didn't want the mood to turn sour again.

After she completed the dishes while he dug for snow gear for both of them, they met in the living room and got dressed. Terry might have a small cabin, but he tucked a lot of things inside for any occasion, it seemed. She had a hat, gloves, boots, and a scarf, but to her surprise and delight, Terry had a pair of snow pants that fit her perfectly. James also found a pair for himself along with a pair of boots that he said were a bit tight but would do.

She didn't ask why he didn't wear his own if he knew he was coming out here. Knowing the way his emotions changed in the blink of an eye, it might bring the mood back down. So she said nothing.

Grabbing her hand, he pulled her into his arms for a scorching kiss that warmed her from head to toe, then guided her outside. The second he opened the door and she stepped outside right behind him, she wished for his lips back upon hers to heat her up.

It was freezing out. It had to be in the single digits, if not below zero with the wind blowing carelessly around.

"It's a lot colder than I expected it'd be," James said with a laugh as he tugged on her arm to follow him.

"But I see we're not turning back around."

His gaze sharpened, his eyes twinkling with merriment. "Oh, we're building a snowman." He stopped about fifteen feet from the cabin, perfectly aligned with the window of the cabin. "We'll build him right here, so he can watch over us."

"Our bodyguard snowman."

"Someone's gotta keep the riffraff away." He chuckled, then his eyes started to fill with disgust as if he was suddenly thinking *he* was the riffraff.

To distract him, not wanting the fun to disappear, she shoved him lightly, but not hard enough that he lost his balance.

His eyes rounded as his mouth fell open in shock.

She didn't wait for his reaction, she bent down and scooped up a pile of soft snow and didn't even take the time to form a ball before tossing it in his direction.

His deep, masculine laughter filled the cold morning air as the snow hit the front of his jacket, touching his face.

"You better run." His brown eyes glittered with mischief and excitement as he scooped a hand full of snow.

She giggled and squealed, turning around to make a run for it, not getting far when a wallop of snow hit her in the back. Bending down, she took an extra second to make a proper snowball this time and turned slightly, aiming in his direction. He already had another snowball prepared, throwing at the same time she did.

They had perfect aim because both snowballs collided with each other in midair.

James held up his gloved hands in surrender. "Truce." A hint of mischief still lingered. "For now."

Erin nodded, laughing. "For now." Getting on her knees,

she smirked teasingly at him. "I bet I make a better snowman than you."

Plopping down into the snow a few feet from her, he winked. "Best snowman wins a massage. Full body massage."

With the icy temperatures filling every vein in her body, the wind whipping, the coldness seeping in from the ground as she sat in the snow, it all drifted away.

Full body massage...

Instant pleasure attacked her.

Giving a wink of her own, she nodded. "Deal."

They both started their task, laughing and jesting with each other as they worked hard on rolling the snow into several balls.

She didn't plan to half-ass anything. She was totally in it to win it. Not that she didn't think if she asked nicely he wouldn't give her a full body massage. She was pretty positive he'd do it anyway, but it didn't mean she wanted to lose.

After getting the bottom snowball as big as she could, she positioned it right in front of the window. She giggled when he brought his snowball over and sighed heavily. His wasn't lined up directly with the window like hers.

Point one to her.

Digging in vigorously on ball number two, she rolled and rolled until it was just under the size of the first one. Not too big, and not too small. As if it were a race to get done first, as well as have the best one, James finished at the same time as her.

Except when she went to lift the ball to place it on top of the bottom one, it proved heavier than she expected. Huffing, she tried again.

"I win if you can't lift it," James snickered jokingly as he lifted his ball without much effort and arranged it on top of the bottom ball.

Eyeing it closely, she decided hers was a lot more round and more proportioned with her first one than his.

She fixed him a firm, determined glare. "I don't give up easily. On anything."

He paused in rolling his last ball, staring quietly at her.

He could take what she said in any way he wanted. As if she were talking about the snowman...or life in general. Maybe even the thing happening between them.

Regardless of how he took it, it was true. She didn't give up.

She wouldn't give up easily on them.

"I want your hands all over me. I'm not losing." He smiled, winked, and went back to rolling his last ball.

Determined more than ever to win because she wanted *his* hands all over her, she tried again to pick up her ball.

Straining, the muscles in her arms screaming, she managed to pick it up and shove it on top of her bottom ball. Except, she must've slammed it harder than she anticipated because a small chunk broke off. Groaning, but refusing defeat, she grabbed some snow and patched the hole as best as she could, smoothing it out as if it never broke to begin with.

Getting on her hands and knees again, she started to form the last ball. Although it wasn't as big as the other two, it was still quite difficult to lift when she finished rolling it into the perfect ball for the head.

Standing back to admire the body of her snowman, who stood about as tall as her, she decided the exertion to build him was worth it. Glancing at James' snowman standing almost as tall as hers, she had to admit his looked nice.

Not as awesome as hers, but he did pretty well. Her balls

were more round and smooth compared to his, which were uneven and not proportioned.

"I'll be right back." James ran into the cabin and came out less than a minute later with the box of hats and scarfs Terry had stocked in the cabin.

As she dug through the box for the perfect outfit for her snowman, she wondered if these things were Terry's son's, the one who died that James had mentioned. She couldn't even imagine how painful it would be to lose a child. Or anyone in her family.

Besides her aunt, who suffered from Alzheimer's, her family hadn't been hit with tragedy much. Everyone was healthy and whole, living life almost as carefree as most people would want.

She really couldn't complain.

Placing a hunter green knit hat on top of her snowman and wrapping a big red scarf around his neck, she walked to the tree line to find more supplies for the rest of her snowman. James followed her path after he placed a black knit hat on top of the snowman's head and an orange scarf around his neck.

She put medium sized sticks for the snowman's arms and used some bark from the tree as his eyes and mouth. James did the same thing.

Then they both took a few steps back and admired the snowmen. As she looked happily at the snowmen standing side by side with two wide bark smiles on their faces and the sticks hanging out almost like they were waving back at them, she thought they both looked pretty damn awesome.

In her book, it was a tie.

James sighed. "I can see the clear winner."

Looking at him with a smile, the cold starting to freeze

her to the bone, she wrapped her arms around her middle and said, "And who is that?"

Meeting her gaze, his eyes filled with bliss, his grin coated with devilish intent, he reached out and circled his gloved hand around her neck, pulling her closer. "You definitely won."

"Really?" she whispered as his lips moved closer to hers. "I bet you're so sad. You were dying to get my hands all over your body."

His lips hovered close to hers. "Actually, I'm looking forward to getting my hands all over your body."

His lips touched hers, warming her instantly. Everything drifted away.

The snow disappeared.

The cold didn't exist.

The troubles in both their lives weren't even a worry.

Wrapping her arms around him, soaking up his strength and comfort, she whispered against his lips in between small kisses, "I'll take that full body massage right now, please."

He surprised her by stepping back and swinging her into his arms.

"Let me warm you up. Your lips are freezing."

Oh, yes. She wanted him to warm her up. Make her forget they'd eventually have to talk about where they were going from here.

Because, even though he planned to leave town, she didn't want to lose him.

She'd leave with him.

If he'd have her.

10

JAMES SNUGGLED Erin tighter into his arms, his back against the couch near the fireplace with Erin in front, her back to his chest. Kissing her on the neck, he inhaled her sweet scent. A mixture of something berry and fruity. Strawberries, maybe.

They had both taken a shower when they came inside, wanting to freshen up from playing in the snow. Although it had been cold, they had exerted a lot of energy making the snowmen. He showered first so he knew the shampoo and conditioner in the bathroom wasn't fruity smelling. When she came out of the bathroom in only a t-shirt, one she must've swiped from his bag, he made her a hot chocolate and then sat with her in front of the fireplace.

Breathing deeply again, he pressed his lips to her slender neck, licking up until he hit her ear where he nibbled. The scent clinging to her delicate body was driving him wild.

Erin sighed as she leaned further into his chest, exposing more of her neck. "What are you doing? I thought we were resting for a while."

His hands tightened on her stomach as his lips caressed her neck and shoulder with more soft kisses. Seeing her in his shirt, hanging sexy and loose around her tiny frame, ramped up his desire for her through the roof. He could've taken her right then and there against the hallway wall. Except she deserved better than a round of rough, dirty sex.

She deserved everything. The world. Her deepest desires. Her every wish.

He wasn't even close to being deserving of someone as pure as her.

But her sweet aroma he kept inhaling was driving his senses wild. He didn't know how much longer he could control himself. His lips tickled her neck again with light, breezy kisses.

"James..."

His name came out of her mouth roughly, a whisper, but with so much ache and need.

Pressing hot, firm kisses up her neck once more to her ear, he lightly bit her earlobe before whispering, "I can't help myself. You smell so delicious. Like a strawberry. I want to eat you up."

A giggle fell from her beautiful lips. "It's just a little body spray I keep in my purse. I didn't know it was so powerful."

His hands squeezed around her stomach, his lips touching her neck one last time. Otherwise, he would lose his control and snap, taking her again in front of the fire. As much as he wanted to do that, he wanted to sit with her and snuggle as well. He didn't want only sex.

"Everything about you is powerful." His voice dropped to a whisper. "You have the power to bring me to my knees with one look, one touch, one word. You own me, Erin. You have for the longest time and just didn't know it."

Her breath hitched, her head turning to look at him.

Reaching up, her hand caressed his cheek. Every time she touched him that way, his heart skipped a beat. She always touched him so softly and tenderly, as if treasuring the moment.

"But I do now."

He grinned, her hand still on his cheek. "What are you going to do with that knowledge?"

Her eyes turned sad for a brief second, so brief he wasn't sure if he misread it. Then a shimmer of desire punctured his aching heart. "Show you the love you deserve. I know you don't think you deserve anything."

His eyes closed as her hand brushed his cheek with such aching tenderness it tore his heart in two. "I don't deserve anything. I definitely don't deserve someone as pure and perfect as you. I don't deserve my sister's forgiveness."

Her head fell against his chest, her body twisted sideways, her hand still holding his cheek. He couldn't open his eyes to see the look in her eyes. No matter what kind of look it might be. He simply couldn't see it.

"Maybe you think you don't deserve your sister's forgiveness, but she's giving it. And you're taking it. As you should." She sighed. "I still haven't apologized to my sister for walking out on her and the things I said." A tortured laugh escaped. "And all over my uncle, a man who didn't deserve me sticking up for him. But in the end, I did it for my aunt."

He opened his eyes, gazing down at her head, but unable to see her eyes with the way she rested against him.

"My uncle moved to this town when we were kids. We heard whispers about why he left, but I never heard he hurt my aunt. Not physically. I guess I never understood how you could hurt someone so badly with only words. I understand now why my dad let him leave without fighting. Why he never made the effort to contact him. But my poor aunt... what about her? Everyone abandoned her."

"Not you."

"As a kid, I did. But yeah, I stepped up as an adult." Another strangled laugh let loose. "For selfish reasons, James. I'm not this perfect woman you have on this pedestal. My uncle reached out to me, out of everyone, to see if I'd help with her care. Probably because I was going through college to become a nurse. He was selfish, too. Although I'll give him credit. He offered to finish paying for my education while I helped him out. But it would've never worked. It's not like I could take night classes. I was in the middle of my clinicals, right in the trenches of getting my degree." She sighed heavily, almost painfully. "I couldn't handle it. I hated it. I want to help people, but I realized not in that way. He gave me a perfect out for my problem. I was able to drop out and quit school with a good excuse, instead of looking like a pathetic dropout."

James kissed the top of her head, embracing her with a comforting squeeze. She might be trying to convince him she wasn't perfect, that she had flaws, but she'd never have the kind of flaws as him. She'd always be perfect in his eyes. Always.

"You can still go back and finish college."

"I don't want to be a nurse. I liked what I did at the hospital. Helping but not *helping*. If that makes sense."

"You *like* it at the hospital. Not liked. You still work there. And I won't let you quit because of me." His tone of voice was almost lethal, letting her know he wouldn't tolerate her quitting. Before she could counter his determination, he said, "And you can still finish college with a different degree. You don't have to go back and be a nurse. You can be anything you want to be."

Her hand, resting on his cheek as if it belonged there all the time, smoothed across his cheek and down his chest. "I don't know what I want to do. That's the problem."

She sat up, looking at him with concern, worry, and what he could only assume was something close to love.

No, affection. That's what it was. Because Erin would never love him. Care about him, sure. Love, no.

"You were kissing me and making me feel good. How did we get on this depressing subject?"

"I have no idea. But—"

Her finger to his lips stopped his words. "Start believing I'm not this perfect woman. See my imperfections. See..." Her voice cracked as her bottom lip trembled. "What do you want from me, James? What do you want after we leave this cabin? What is this? Is this a fantasy until the real world intrudes?"

Each and every question gutted him straight to the core. Ripped his heart out. Twisted his insides to such an extreme he thought he was going to get sick.

"I want..." He hesitated. "I want this fantasy to live on... even when we leave this cabin." His eyes fell, the pain attacking him so strongly he wanted to cry. And damn it, he wouldn't cry in front of her. "But it's not possible."

"Why not? You don't want the town to see us together?"

His gaze flew to hers. "It's for your protection. They'd crucify you. They'd talk about you behind your back, and it wouldn't be nice things. I'm a lo—"

He groaned in pain when Erin bent down and bit his shoulder.

"I'll bite you harder if you call yourself a loser again."

Rubbing his shoulder, a chuckle filled the tiny space between them before he could stop it. "I forgot you threatened that." His eyes twinkled with desire. "I like it when you bite me. That was hard, though."

"It'll only get harder. Don't put yourself down. Don't let the town control your decisions. Do you want me?" She cupped his face with her hands, holding him firmly. "Do you want me, James? All of me? Not just a quick round of sex in a cabin during a blizzard."

Splaying his hands across her back, pulling her closer, his lips mere inches from hers, he nodded. "I want you, Erin. All of you."

Their lips connected.

Words ceased to exist as the heat between them soared even higher than the fire blazing next to them.

11

FOLDING his arms tighter around his beautiful wife, he knew it would be hard not to worry about her when he left.

"Do you have to go so soon? You were working late into the morning and you only had four hours of sleep. It's only lunchtime. Maybe you can get a few more hours of sleep and then go in."

Aiden kissed the top of Theresa's head, then shifted away so he could look her in the eyes. "The roads are still terrible, and people don't have the sense to stay home." He shook his head, his eyes wide with confusion. "Most of the town closed down because of the weather, so they have no reason to go out. Bentley's going back in, too. I have to go." He brushed his lips with hers. "I won't worry as much knowing you're staying home."

"I won't go anywhere. I promise."

"You better not." He used the sternest gaze he owned, then chuckled when she stuck her tongue out.

The laughter in her eyes died as her mouth fell into a frown. "I tried calling James. The call wouldn't go through."

"He's fine. He's at the cabin, and he's fine."

A shiver rippled throughout her body. "I might've..." She blew out a breath. "I might've told Erin where he was. She wasn't answering her phone either. It wouldn't go through."

Well, that was unexpected. Why would Erin want to see James? And why would Theresa tell her when James specifically asked her not to tell anyone?

"Then they must be together. They're both fine. James would never let anything happen to Erin."

A tiny smile filtered out, sending happiness straight to his heart. He hated when his wife looked sad. And the last few months, trying to get pregnant, she always had a sadness filling her eyes.

"Thank you, Aiden."

Frowning, a low chuckle released as he kissed her. "For what?"

"For caring about James when he doesn't always make it easy to like him. For having faith in him that he's a good person. He is. He just loses his way sometimes."

Tightening his hands on her back in comfort, his insides twisted with unease that he had to leave. He didn't want to leave her when she was feeling down.

"He's your brother. That makes him my family, too. No question. In fact," a strangled smile, something close to a frown, punctured his lips, "I called Chief Duncan about what happened at the hospital."

Her eyes narrowed. "Why?"

He smoothed his hands up and down her back, to reassure her, to calm the sudden anger he could see building. "For James. They fired him for something he didn't do. Yes, I believe that." He cocked a brow. "And they're not pressing charges? That's odd. Chief Duncan thought so, too. He's going to have a word with Dr. Pearson as soon as the weather clears up."

She trembled. "Are you sure that was the right thing to do?"

"He didn't do anything, Theresa. Right?" Doubt started to trickle in. "Did he tell you something?"

Her eyes widened. "No! He didn't do it. It's just..." She sighed heavily. "Nothing ever goes right for him. What happens if this makes the situation worse and they do decide to press charges?"

"Then we hire him the best damn lawyer there is and fight it. I'm a cop. I trust in the law. And I don't believe in punishing an innocent man. Yes, James can be an asshole." He chuckled to lighten the blow of disrespecting her brother. "But not every family is perfect, and I won't turn my back on him. Because you won't either. And I will always do anything to make you happy. That's what's important to me."

Her head fell against his chest, her hands squeezing the back of his uniform. "You're amazing. You have no idea how much I love you."

He embraced her harder, soaking up her warmth and her love. "I do know. Because I love you the same, if not more."

Glancing out the sliding glass doors in the dining room, he wished the snow would stop. Over fifteen inches had fallen since yesterday evening, the wind blowing up to thirty-five miles per hour in some areas, creating almost whiteout conditions. It had been dangerous working last night, hazardous conditions for even him and all the other emergency crews. But people needed help. They would today as well, as the snow continued to fall; at least another two to three inches had accumulated so far. They were predicting another five to six inches before the snow would stop. The wind gusted with a vengeance, blowing the snow all around like a mini tornado.

He didn't want to leave Theresa. Not because it was dangerous out there, but because...

Just because.

His wife needed him.

"Stop. I can feel you worrying in my arms."

Tiny laughter floated out as he kissed the top of her head. "You're in *my* arms, sweetheart. And I'll always worry about you. Especially right now. I wish I could help James right this minute for you."

But it was a waiting game. Until the snow stopped and the roads were cleared. As soon as that happened, he'd drive out to the cabin to check on James, regardless of how he'd react. Theresa was worried about him, so that's all he needed to know.

James and Erin were out in the middle of nowhere with a blizzard in their midst. They could've lost power.

Shit.

He hoped they didn't.

Kissing the top of her head again, pressing his lips there for a few seconds, he strengthened his grip. "I should go. When the snow stops, I'll check on James. I'll make sure he's okay." A low groan escaped when he felt tears soak the front of his shirt. "We'll help him. Don't worry, sweetheart. He'll be okay."

Because Aiden wouldn't accept any other option.

He'd do anything to keep his wife happy and the tears at bay. She had cried too much over the past few months, and he didn't want to see any more tears. They broke his heart every time.

Like now.

He'd fix this.

———

ERIN'S FINGERS sunk into the curtain, curling her hand into a tight fist, as she stared out into the night watching the snow fall.

Her body was coiled taut with a mixture of tension and pleasure. Half of her wanted to go into the kitchen and have her dirty way with James again. Because the two other times they had sex, once in the morning, once after playing outside, wasn't enough. Her body still tingled with the after-effects of his soft touch, his warm caresses, his gentle kisses.

The other half wanted to smack him on the back of the head for continuing to think he was a loser. That they couldn't be together because of what the town would say.

She didn't care.

People could say what they wanted to say. It would never change how she felt about him. How she loved him.

A whisper of a smile touched her lips as she looked at the two snowmen they made earlier stand side by side.

She could still see the joy spread across his face, the bright, beautiful smile that lit up his features, the happiness sparkling in his eyes. They both had so much fun creating two silly snowmen.

When was the last time James had fun? Real, honest fun?

She imagined it had been a long time, especially when most of the town didn't converse with him. Oh, they could pull together in a pinch and help people out, but they could also show how cruel and evil they could be to each other. Ignoring James as he mopped the floor. Not even looking him in the eye as they passed by. Pretending he didn't exist as he emptied the trash cans. Not even acknowledging with a simple *thank you* as he held the door open for them.

She wasn't blind. She saw every slight toward him. So rude.

And why?

Because he had a problem that he admitted to and got help for. That was a lot better than some people she knew.

A cupboard door shut with a loud bang, turning her attention to the kitchen. Hard concentration swamped James' face as he poured some kind of liquid in a bowl, then started to whisk it in a smooth circular motion.

He looked like a pro chef, so familiar cooking and creating masterpieces. So far they had eaten simple stuff, but masterpieces, nonetheless. A small sandwich, an easy breakfast with eggs and toast, a delicious cup of hot chocolate, a can of chicken noodle soup. Every meal and drink he had prepared was perfection. Her tastebuds started to salivate, wondering what he was making them for supper.

Her lips arched up with fascination as she watched him dig in another cupboard. He grabbed something, some kind of spice, then swung the cupboard shut with a light touch, yet it closed with a soft bang. His movements were fluid, precise. Like he knew the cabin well and could cook in his sleep.

And although his concentration was fierce, she saw the contentment in his gaze as he prepared the meal with finesse.

He was enjoying himself.

He clearly liked to cook.

Turning back to the window, the glittery white snow falling peacefully outside, she tried to decide what to do.

Continue to argue with him that they were meant to be

together? Or let it go and make a grand display in front of the town to show him it didn't matter to her?

Three days until Christmas.

Only two days left in the cabin.

Her hand tightened around the curtain.

Unless they spent Christmas here together. Alone. Just the two of them. The outside world far away where nobody could disrupt the desire and love building between them.

Sighing, she knew that would never happen. James would be spending Christmas with Theresa.

She was supposed to make an appearance at her uncle's house. Not something she looked forward to, but for her aunt, she'd show up.

The tiny bubble she wanted to create wasn't possible. She'd have to face the real world eventually.

Warm hands slid around her waist, a hard body to her back, then soft lips touched her neck. Leaning back into James' embrace, she closed her eyes as he peppered a few more kisses along her neck.

"See anything interesting out there?"

Her eyes opened, a smile spreading across her face. "More snow."

Chuckling, he nuzzled his nose against her neck, then pressed another tender kiss. "I can't believe it's still snowing. I swear two feet had to have fallen already. We might never get out of here."

Her hand clutched the curtain. *If only.* "Would that be such a bad thing?"

"Just you and me? Alone?" Another kiss hit her neck. "That's never a bad thing. Erin..."

His voice trailed off as if he were afraid to keep talking. She even felt a slight tremble in his body, even though his grip around her waist didn't falter.

"What are you cooking?"

"Something delicious."

"Which is?" she asked with a light airy laugh.

A nibble touched her ear. "A surprise."

The laughter in his tone settled her aching heart down. She hated when she heard the hesitancy in his voice, the pain etched in each syllable. She wanted to ask what he wanted to say, but after changing the subject and getting the lightheartedness back in his tone, she didn't want to ruin the mood.

"Give me a hint."

His hands grasped her hips, pulling her back against his hard erection she could feel against her butt. "No hints."

Another kiss hit her neck. "A tiny hint?"

A low groan slipped from his lips as his grip on her hips strengthened. "You're..."

He still wanted to tell her something, but struggled to get the words out. Did she want to know what he had to say?

She remained silent, hoping he'd find the nerve to tell her. Also dreading when he did.

Another guttural groan escaped. "You're more amazing than I realized. I don't deserve you."

"James—"

"It's the truth, Erin. I don't." His lips scorched her skin with another hard, explosive kiss to her neck. "The thought of leaving this cabin and never seeing you again, never holding you in my arms, never laughing with you, never playing in the snow and watching the happiness spark in your eyes..." He exhaled as if preparing his next words carefully. "The mere thought is like a big gaping hole in my chest. It's like I can't breathe. I can't find the strength to draw in a small ounce of air with the thought of losing you."

"You don't have to," she whispered.

"I know. But it's a fear I can't control. I can't stop telling myself we should never see each other when we leave."

She let the curtain go and twisted around in his arms. Pressing her hands against his chest, she curled her hands into tight fists as she grabbed his shirt, tugging him closer.

"What are you so afraid of? I'm a strong woman. I can handle anything."

His eyes glittered with pain, so deep, so thick with agony, she was afraid he was so far gone in his fear nothing she did or said would save him from himself.

"James?"

But she refused to let his fear win. She would push and push and push until he exploded if she had to.

"I'm afraid...that I'll hurt you." His forehead rested against hers, his voice lowering. "Like I hurt everyone else in my life. I couldn't bear it if I hurt you, too."

"You're hurting me now." He stood tall and tried to back away, but the grip she had on his shirt was strong. "I don't mean physically. Not giving us a chance is hurting me."

He relaxed, but only slightly. Then his lips touched hers with a gentle caress. "I made you supper."

A giggle released. "Wow, way to change the subject with something I already know."

He joined in with her tiny laughter. "What I meant was I made you supper, a fancy supper," he rolled his eyes, "well, as fancy as I can here. I'm trying...I want to show..." He blew out a heavy breath.

Loosening her hands, she reached up and cupped his cheek. "You're the sweetest man I've ever known. And being in this cabin is the best moment of my life."

A sexy, sweet grin punctured his lips. "So, impressing you with my cooking skills is working?"

She chuckled, playfully shrugging. "Well, I haven't tried this mysterious meal yet."

He laughed with her, then his smile disappeared as the sorrow entered his eyes once again.

Her hand brushed his cheek. "Don't. Stay happy. Please."

"I have one more thing to say. I just..." He blew out another breath. "It's a hard one."

"Just say it. Like ripping a bandaid off. Do it quick."

He barely nodded as a speck of a grin emerged. "Do you want to spend Christmas with me? Join me at my sister's house." His chest heaved up and down as if he had just finished a marathon.

Oh.

Wow.

She didn't expect that.

Then his features fell into horror when she didn't respond.

How could she?

She was rendered speechless. Never in a million years did she think he'd invite her over for Christmas with his sister.

It spoke volumes.

It said so many things.

It said one important thing.

He cared. He cared quite a lot. Perhaps even loved her.

His face twisted with pain as she remained silent. The words were there, right on the tip of her tongue, but she couldn't find her voice.

"I knew it."

Before she could find her voice, he shoved out of her arms and walked away.

JAMES STALKED to the kitchen and started to grab the dirty dishes to clean up the mess from a meal meant to impress Erin. Obviously, nothing would impress her. Nothing he did would change the fact that he didn't deserve her and she'd never be his.

She could say whatever she wanted. That she wanted to be with him outside of this cabin. That she wanted the town to see they were a couple.

But did she?

He finally found the nerve to ask her to join him at his sister's for Christmas, and she was so repulsed by the idea she couldn't even say no. The twisted look of disgust on her face had been answer enough.

Lies.

Everything she told him was lies. She only wanted sex with him where no one could see her with him.

Because he was the loser of the town.

The idiot who always made mistakes.

The brother who hurt his sister by stealing from her. By letting his friend almost kill her.

Dropping the dirty bowl and spoon into the sink, he turned on the water, letting it run until it turned hot. Scalding hot. He needed to feel some pain right now.

Because the only thing besides a deep heartache tearing him apart inside, he was feeling the intense urge for a drink.

Good thing there wasn't any alcohol nearby.

He turned off the faucet, flinching when he tried to put his hand into the hot water. He jumped when a hand touched his shoulder. Whirling around, he winced at the agony in Erin's eyes. Did he hurt her when he jumped and turned toward her? Or was this another kind of pain?

Why would she be hurting? He was the one who asked

her to join him for Christmas and she turned him down. *He* was the one hurting.

"James, stop walking away from me."

He shrugged. "I didn't think we had anything left to talk about."

"I didn't even get a chance to answer you."

His eyes narrowed, his voice filled with anger and annoyance. "I heard your answer loud and clear."

Her hands went to her hips as her expression turned defiant and stern. "Is that right? Because I don't recall speaking one word."

"You didn't need words to say no."

Sadness touched her eyes. "I'm saying yes, you big dumbie. I would love to join you at your sister's for Christmas."

He turned back around to the sink, dipping his hands in the burning water, his lips twisting from the pain. "I don't need your fake sympathy. I don't need your lies."

Flinching—again—when her hand landed on his shoulder, he refused to look her way. "You don't need soap to wash dishes either?"

"What?" He met her gaze, one filled with sorrow and concern.

Her gaze traveled to the water where his hands sat submerged. "You have dirty dishes. You have," her brows pleated together, "what looks like very hot water with the way your hands look red and the wince on your face. But you have no soap. I guess you're a miracle worker like that. You can magically turn dishes clean without dish soap."

He couldn't suppress the tiny grin as he glanced at the water. "Well, you only need water. Soap adds some extra cleanliness to it, but water does the trick. Can't get the dirt and grime off without washing it off with water."

"Now that we just had a silly conversation," she said as she let go of his shoulder and pulled his hands out of the scalding water, "are you ready to meet this head-on? Stop running from me."

He didn't want to look at her. But he had no choice when she squeezed his red hands hard, forcing him to meet her gaze, twisting his body so he was looking at her.

"I'm not running."

An eyebrow arched as a devilish smile touched her lips. "Every time you walk away from me, you're running."

He shrugged again, unsure of what she wanted from him. He was looking at her. He was talking to her. He wasn't running right now. But he refused to put his heart on the line again for her to tear it into pieces.

"We've been teetering on the edge of...something for the past day." Her smile turned sweet as desire filtered into her emerald green eyes. "You shocked me, James. It's that simple. I never imagined you'd want to spend Christmas with me because you're so adamant that the town shouldn't see us together. You just shocked me." She tightened her grip on his hands. "But I'd love to come. I want to come with you." Her lips fell into a frown. "And I've never lied to you. Ever."

Okay. So maybe he overreacted.

Maybe.

It was hard to trust when not many people cared about him.

"Does the offer still stand, or did I ruin my chances when words failed to come? Haven't you ever been rendered speechless?"

Yeah, he had.

Right now would classify him as being speechless. He was hearing her words. He was almost believing them. He barely got the words out the first time due to his fear so ingrained in his mind, he didn't think he'd get them out again. Especially with the fear tripled ten times over because she ignored him the first time.

Her beautiful, sweet smile stayed in place as she waited for him to answer.

This was why he had to trust her.

Because this was Erin.

Sweet, delicate, lovely Erin.

Never in his life had she been cruel or mean, or said things behind his back. She was always a good friend, talking to him, smiling and laughing, treating him with respect, even knowing the kind of screw up he was.

"James…" Her smile started to falter. "Please tell me I didn't ruin my chances. Please."

"You—"

Words failed when the entire cabin went dark.

He felt her but could hardly see even with the light coming from the fireplace in the living room as Erin stepped into his arms and held him tightly. "Did we just lose power?"

Yeah, they lost power.

"We did."

As she trembled in his arms, whether from the darkness surrounding them, or the issues between them, he knew one thing for sure.

He lost his heart to her.

She had his heart and soul.

No matter how badly his fear consumed him, he had to power through this and take what she offered when she offered it.

His lips found her neck in the dark. "You didn't ruin your chances. I'm sorry for walking away and the things I said. This isn't easy for me."

"We'll muddle through this thing together."

He smiled at her quiet words, then pressed another kiss to her neck.

Now, about the electricity.

That was a problem he had to fix. Very soon, or they'd freeze to death.

12

His hand grasped the handle of the door hard, his brows scrunching with concern. Not that Erin could see how worried he was. But, in case she could, he was trying his hardest to hide it. "Go sit by the fire until I get back."

She tugged on his arm, her face inching closer to his where he could see the worry in her eyes, even as dark as the cabin was. "Maybe I should go with. It could be a two-person job. Are you sure Terry has a generator?"

"I don't know. The shed is on the side of the cabin. I'll take a look and check things out." Cupping his hand around her neck, he pulled her closer and placed a light kiss to her lips. "I want you to stay here. Be careful, but check the cupboard by the fridge. I think there are some candles and matches. Maybe a flashlight or two. Then, please," his hand caressed the back of her neck, "go sit by the fire and stay warm."

She kissed his lips. "Okay, James. Be quick. I don't want you to get too cold."

He nodded, then let go of her and opened the door, stepping outside into the brutal winter night. Snow lightly fell, coating the ground in a thick blanket of white. He had bundled up as he had when they played in the snow earlier in the day, but since the night had descended, the temperature had significantly dropped.

Brutally cold didn't even begin to describe it.

He pulled out the flashlight he found in a drawer in the kitchen and flipped the switch. It didn't provide much light, but it was enough to help him.

Trudging through the deep snow, he made his way to the side of the cabin. Why couldn't the power have gone out after the pasta dish he prepared finished baking in the oven? It wasn't anything fancy. Just some noodles, ground beef, a can of diced tomatoes, and cheese with a few spices tossed in to make a gourmet Hamburger Helper.

He had hoped to impress Erin, show her that he wasn't a complete imbecile. He knew how to cook. He knew how to take care of himself. He didn't do TV dinners every night.

He was trying.

Trying to be the kind of man she deserved.

That's all he wanted to prove.

Laughter filled the night air as he took the shed key out of his pocket and fiddled with the lock. Proving he was man enough for her by making a dumb meal. Maybe he *was* an idiot. It sounded so stupid now that he thought about it. With the power going out, it didn't matter anymore.

Unless he found a generator and got it running. Then he could continue his lame attempt at impressing Erin that he might be worthy of her.

The lock popped open, but when he tried to remove the key, it slipped from his gloved hands into the snow.

"Shit." A strangled laugh floated out. "Always causing problems, James. That's what you're good at."

Shaking his head at his idiocy for losing the key, he

opened the shed door. He'd come back out here to dig for it when they weren't on the cusp of freezing to death. If he couldn't find it, he'd buy Terry a new lock and key.

Shining the light inside the shed, he stepped in, shifting it back and forth, looking for his prize.

After walking around the entire shed, which didn't take many footsteps since it was a pretty small area, James kicked a shovel.

It slammed against the ground, hitting the lawnmower.

No generator.

Walking out of the shed, he shut the door and looked around. All he could see was darkness and lots and lots of white.

In a way, it was beautiful. The snow covering the ground, looking soft and inviting. He imagined Erin's excitement this afternoon as they built their snowmen. She'd have fun coming out here playing in it again. Maybe making snow angels, or playing the game cut the pie. Or even having a snowball fight.

He and his sister had so much fun playing outside in the snow when they were kids—when life wasn't filled with pain and sadness because his dad liked to drink too much.

Conjuring old memories wasn't going to help him. Neither was thinking that playing in the snow would be a good idea. It might put a smile on Erin's face, but it would also be extremely cold and they only had a small fire to keep them warm.

Hiking back to the front of the cabin in the deep snow, he soaked up the little warmth that was left as soon as he stepped inside.

Erin stood up by the fire. "Any luck?"

James shook his head, then realized she probably

couldn't see him all too well. "No. Terry was pretty prepared for everything, but didn't have a generator."

Glancing to the corner of the room where a large pile of wood sat, he knew they'd be okay for the night. But their little haven away from the world would end tomorrow. They couldn't stay here without power.

He shed off his boots and snow gear and carried them close to the fire, laying them out to dry overnight—hopefully.

"We'll stay by the fire tonight, and then tomorrow we'll walk to our cars."

A brow popped up on her beautiful, concerned face. "Which are probably stuck even more in the snow."

James' shoulders slumped, then he straightened his spine. He couldn't let Erin see any weakness. If he couldn't impress her with his cooking, he'd have to impress her with his courage and strength. He would keep her safe. He would take care of her.

Rubbing his hands near the fire, he made sure to look her in the eyes. "Maybe so, but we'll get better reception to call for help. I'll call Theresa to have Aiden pick us up. It wouldn't hurt to see if we have reception now."

Walking to the kitchen, he grabbed his phone from the table and tried to call his sister. The call wouldn't go through.

"No reception. We'll have to walk to the road tomorrow." He glanced at Erin. He could see her gorgeous face, her body illuminated by the firelight, haloing her like the angel she was. "We'll be okay, Erin. I'll get you home."

"I know you will." Her lips curled into a sweet smile. "Now come join me by the fire. You have to be freezing after being outside. The best way to warm up is by body heat."

That wasn't something he could argue with. He met her

by the fire, pulling her into his arms. "We should pull more blankets out of the bedroom."

"We should eat something, too," she said quietly as she pulled his shirt up and over his head.

Cold air rushed over his skin, making him shiver.

Her hands rubbed up and down his chest, making another tremble coat his body.

"You're freezing, James."

He pulled off her shirt, tugging her closer. "No, I'm definitely not cold. I have a beautiful woman in my arms warming me up."

Kissing her hard on the lips, their tongues tangling, low moans filling the cabin, he cursed the power for ruining part of the night. But it didn't ruin all of it because he still had Erin in his arms. At the moment, that's all that mattered.

They both shed their clothes quickly, suddenly needing each other with a mad frenzy. Cuddling under the few blankets they had, James touched her most sensitive spot with his fingers as his lips devoured her mouth. He might've been cold from being outside, but it didn't take much to warm him up. Erin in his arms was all the heat he needed. And she was right. Body heat was the best way to warm up.

His lips started trailing light kisses across her face and to her neck as his fingers worked their magic, Erin twisting and moaning under him.

"James..."

Pressing soft, tender kisses along her neck, making a pathway to her ear, he nibbled before whispering, "Yes, sweetheart. Tell me what you want."

Plunging a finger inside her, rubbing and pleasuring her with finesse, he playfully bit her ear. "Tell me, Erin. Tell me what you want."

Her hands scratched down his back as her lips attached to his shoulder, biting down as an orgasm suddenly ripped through her system.

Some pain but also lots of pleasure coursed through his veins as her teeth sunk into his skin. He never knew a bite could be such a kick to his system. It made him crave, yearn, beg for more.

"I need you." His lips refused to disengage from her neck, licking, caressing, kissing, as his hand fumbled around the floor for the extra condoms lying around.

"I need you more," she whispered, her hands running up and down his back, soothing, yet urging him to go faster.

He highly doubted that. He'd always need her more.

Lifting his body slightly, he put on the condom, then entered her with one swift stroke. He stilled for a moment, enjoying the sweet sensation of being buried deep inside her.

"James..."

Every time she uttered his name with such abandoned passion, he wanted to do something to make her say it again and again and again. His name on her lips was like an aphrodisiac.

He started moving, thrusting hard and deep. Erin matched his pace, her hands clutching his back, urging him on even faster.

The fire, the heat, the want and burning need between them was enough to warm him up. He didn't need anything else to make him feel better from the brutal cold outside.

Pumping harder, low groans mingled with kisses on her neck, he felt himself rising to an orgasm so strong he wasn't sure he'd have the energy to get up afterward and get more blankets.

"More, James."

Yes.

More.

More of her. More of them. More of everything.

"James..."

Just the sound of his name whispered on her lips once again was enough to send him over the edge. He jerked hard one more time, tensing, the bliss pulsating through his veins. Erin lightly bit down on his shoulder again, intensifying the ecstasy splintering throughout his body.

He collapsed onto her, the energy to move too much effort. But he didn't want to crush her. He started to roll to the side, but her hands tightening on his back stalled him.

"Don't move. Keep warming me up. I'm cold."

Pressing a kiss to her neck, he chuckled. "I will warm you up until you're not cold anymore."

"I don't think you can ever move because I have a feeling I'm going to be cold all night."

The truth was in those words, even though she meant it teasingly. They would be cold all night. But not cold enough to freeze to death as long as he kept the fire blazing, retrieved more blankets from the bedroom, and held her close in his arms.

It was going to be a long night.

Lifting his head to look into her brilliant green eyes, he kissed her lips.

But it was going to be a long pleasurable night with Erin in his arms.

13

THE FIRST THING that woke him up was the shiver that touched Erin. Curled into his embrace, sleeping deeply, nothing should've made her shiver.

The second thing that woke him up was the blast of cold air to his face when he shifted away from the dying fire.

He slept lightly most of the night, getting out of their warm cocoon to make sure the fire never died and they didn't freeze to death. Straining his neck, he looked at the clock above the mantel. He had been out the past four hours. Obviously in a very deep sleep, he felt out of it.

Blinking a few times, trying to get rid of the sleepiness that wanted to take control, he kissed the side of Erin's head. He should crawl out from under the big pile of covers and get ready to leave. The moment he did, he'd get more than a blast of coldness—he'd get a torrential downpour threatening to freeze his entire body in one move. Frozen like a statue.

Snuggling closer to Erin, nuzzling his lips on her neck, he planted a light kiss. Then he paused as he eyed the love bite—as she liked to call them—on her shoulder.

The last time he saw that, he fled the room, hating himself for hurting her. This time, he hugged her tighter, kissing the spot with a tenderness that he hoped would make the mark go away. Of course, it didn't.

Besides having a simple sandwich, since he couldn't finish his pasta dish, they talked throughout the night bundled under the thick fort of blankets. And when he couldn't take the torture of just holding her in his arms, he loved her body. Kissing, caressing, and memorizing every inch.

It could be the last time he ever held her in his arms. They had to leave today. Head to the road and find a good signal to call for help.

She said she wanted to be with him. She said she didn't care what the town said.

He still wasn't sure he wanted her to ruin her reputation for him. He was a lo—

Stopping that train of thought, already hearing Erin's stern voice telling him to knock it off, he repeated in his mind several times he was good enough. He was good enough for her.

If only he could believe it.

His hand splayed across her stomach moved to her breast, fondling with a sweet caress, as he pressed his lips to her neck again.

He wanted to love her body one more time.

She moaned at his soft touch.

But they couldn't. They had to get going before the coldness seeping into the cabin really started to get to them. If he wouldn't have let the fire die out, he could've loved her one more time. He just had to hope he'd be seeing her again once they left the cabin.

"James…"

Her quiet voice, whispering his name so erotically, turned him hard as a rock, harder than before. It was almost too much to control himself.

"Don't say my name like that. Things are liable to happen," he whispered with a growl, then kissed her neck.

Sweet laughter filled the icy-cold cabin as she opened her eyes. "Then don't entice me. My face feels like it's going to fall off."

"I didn't wake up to stoke the fire. I was out of it. It's nearly dead. We should go."

Wrapping her arms around him, increasing her hold, she shivered again. "I don't want to leave. I like this alone time with you."

"Me, too." He let out a silent sigh, his heart suddenly pounding. "Maybe we can…we can…you know…retry that meal I tried to make…at…one of our places."

Wow. That sounded terrible. He couldn't even speak in a coherent sentence. He sounded like an idiot. And he should've said his place, but he didn't exactly live in the best part of town, and the place he rented wasn't much to talk about.

He was embarrassed. He didn't want Erin to see where he lived and realize how wrong he was for her.

Peeking her hand out from underneath the covers, she cupped his cheek as another sharp tremble coated her body. "I like that idea. Wherever you are is where I want to be." The pressure on his cheek intensified. "Because we're spending the holidays together, right?"

He kissed her hard, answering her fear with as much reassurance as he could. "Right."

He had the same fear rushing through his veins. He

didn't want to lose her so soon, but he was a realist. It was going to happen whether he wanted it to or not. Nothing good ever lasted in his life.

"Let's get dressed, pick up, and head out of here. We don't need to do a thorough cleaning. I'll come back another day." Not to mention he had to attempt to find the key for the shed he lost last night.

They kissed one more time, deep and slow, as if savoring the way they tasted together. So right and delicious.

Hating to do it, he disengaged from her and slid out from under the covers. The cold air wrapped around him like a tight band, threatening to suffocate him.

"Shit! It's cold. Be quick, Erin. I don't want any of your fingers to fall off." He said it with a smile as he whipped on his pants. He was joking, of course. Mostly. The cabin was filled with so much cold air, it felt like they spent the night outside. It wasn't out of the realm of possibility to develop frostbite if they didn't get moving and out of here.

They dressed with speed as if they were about to be caught by unsuspecting parents. James shoved his few belongings he brought with him into his duffle bag, Erin doing the same, then grabbed two granola bars from the cupboard and two bottles of water from the fridge.

They ate the granola bars, tossed the garbage away, then prepared for the brutal coldness that was about to slap them in the face as soon as they stepped outside.

Erin put her phone in her jacket pocket, zipping it up, then shoved on her large winter gloves. "Hopefully we get lucky and find some reception soon. I hate to think we'll get to the cars and still not have any and have to walk even further."

After putting on his gloves, he brushed his hand behind her neck, which was snuggled with a thick scarf around it.

Kissing her tenderly, he smiled, hoping to ease her worries. Hoping to ease some of his, too. "I'll get you home. I promise." His smile turned into a devious grin. "Then I'll really warm you up."

Biting her bottom lip as a smile peeked through, she giggled. "I'm holding you to that."

Grabbing their bags, they headed outside. James' entire body shuddered from the sharp sting of the cold as it wrapped around him. He saw Erin shiver just as hard as he fumbled with the key in his gloved hand and locked the door. After shoving the key into his jacket pocket and zipping it up, he grabbed her hand and started walking toward the road. It'd be at least a mile walk, trudging through the deep, thick snow. Thank goodness for the trees lining the path, otherwise, he probably would've gotten turned around. Everything lay blanketed in a smooth white picture. Snow coated the ground and trees everywhere. He made sure to keep him and Erin in the middle of the road, as some of the branches on the trees looked heavy with snow. As if one small gust of wind would have it come crashing down on their heads, burying them alive.

He promised Erin he'd get her home, and he'd keep that promise, even if he got hurt in the process.

"It's so pretty."

James squeezed her hand as he grinned. "Yeah, it is." Then he chuckled. "We didn't even say goodbye to our snowmen."

She laughed, her eyes twinkling with delight. "Well, when you come back to straighten up, I'll come with and say a proper goodbye with you."

His heart skipped a beat. He knew she was talking about the snowmen, but it felt strangely like...

Forcing the smile to stay on his face, he averted his gaze,

focusing straight ahead. He would not lose her. He had to keep repeating it to believe it.

"James…" She tugged on his hand. "Are you okay?"

Erin was too damn perceptive. "I'm fine. I want to get somewhere warm." She might've deciphered his mood change, but he wasn't going to admit it.

She tugged sharply on his hand again.

"Erin, I said—"

"I heard you." She stopped walking, her face full of concentration. "Not that I believe you, but that's not why I tugged on your hand again. Do you hear that?"

James looked around as he strained to listen. In the distance, he heard a low roar. Almost like it belonged to a snowmobile.

When a dark shape started to form ahead, curving around the bend in the road, he couldn't believe his eyes. It *was* a snowmobile.

Two of them.

They stopped a few feet from them, both drivers popping off at the same time. Aiden removed his helmet first. The second driver turned out to be his friend Bentley.

"You okay?" Aiden asked, glancing between him and Erin. Although, his question had seemed more directed at him rather than Erin. For some odd reason, that made him feel marginally better. As if Aiden knew he'd keep Erin safe.

He nodded. "We're fine. We lost power last night. We had to stay close to the fireplace during the night. We decided to head to our cars, try to get a signal to call you."

"A few other places in this area lost power. Not many houses around here, but enough to notify the electric company. We figured so did you." Bentley smiled as if they were friends or something. Which they weren't. He barely talked to the guy other than saying *hello* in passing.

Bentley was one of the few that actually acknowledged him. Most people ignored him when he was near as if he were contagious with a deadly disease.

"Theresa's been worried about you." A crooked grin touched Aiden's lips. "So have I."

Again, for some odd reason, James believed him. That Aiden wasn't giving him a line simply because he was married to his sister.

"I appreciate you coming to check on us. It's damn cold out."

"Well, let's go." Bentley waved a hand to follow as he hopped back on his snowmobile.

Remembering Erin's confession about having had a crush on Aiden, he nodded toward Bentley. "You ride with him. I'll ride with Aiden."

A knowing smile splintered across her face. "Of course." Then to his surprise, she pulled him closer, pressing a sweet kiss to his lips. "You're the only one for me," she whispered. "I don't have a crush on Aiden anymore."

He kissed her harder, not caring what those two thought. Because clearly Erin didn't care, announcing what had transpired between them without blinking an eye. "You're still riding with Bentley."

She nodded, giving him a seductive wink, then crawled onto the snowmobile behind Bentley, grabbing the helmet he offered her. James took a seat behind Aiden, also taking the helmet he had waiting for him.

A low chuckle rented the air in front of him. "So, I guess you had a nice time in the cabin?"

"Shut up, Officer Crowl."

Aiden turned his head, a wily smile plastered on his face. "It's Aiden, James. When I give you shit about a woman as a brother does, it's Aiden." Then he popped his helmet on.

Well...

He didn't know how to respond to that.

A brother?

Like he cared?

Yeah, he had no words.

14

ERIN TOOK off her jacket and handed it to Theresa, who looked concerned yet happy all in one. She kept glancing between her and James, probably dying to ask what transpired between them but too polite to ask.

Aiden had wanted to drop off the snowmobiles at his home before bringing her home. She understood. Why lug the machines all through town when they were passing their house anyway? And why give the town something to talk about? Or have them ask why Aiden and Bentley needed the snowmobiles in the first place.

Bookers Road had been plowed a few times, but not enough. It hadn't been easy to drive on. Aiden and Bentley had to park their truck quite a bit away from the cabin, which made using the snowmobiles a very smart choice. Erin doubted they would've even managed to find a signal at the road. She and James would've been walking a long time before help would've arrived.

Theresa offered her a seat, smiling at James as she pointed toward the couch where a large fluffy blanket lay waiting to snuggle under.

"I'll make you some coffee or hot chocolate." Theresa tilted her head to the side, the same silly smile plastered on her face. "Something to warm you up."

James took a seat first, grabbing her hand to sit next to him. Erin swore Theresa's smile brightened so much it almost hurt her eyes. "Thanks, Tessie. Coffee sounds great."

Even if Theresa did make it into sludge, Erin agreed. Coffee sounded fantastic. And while hot chocolate would do the job as well, she only wanted James to make her hot chocolate. That was *his* thing.

"You probably didn't eat either. I'll whip up a quick breakfast while the coffee brews." A wry smile twisted her lips. "Aiden bought me one of those fancy coffee machines last year for Christmas, so don't worry, it's hard for me to screw up the coffee making at home."

Theresa walked out of the room.

Erin snuggled into James' embrace as he arranged the thick blanket around them, his arm tugging her closer.

"Are you mad at me?"

James' hand stilled from rubbing her arm up and down. "Odd question. Why would I be mad at you?"

Turning to meet his chocolate brown gaze, she shrugged. "For kissing you in front of Aiden. I didn't think about how that would look and—"

His lips met hers, cutting off any further words. "We both agreed we wanted to keep seeing each other outside of the cabin. That you were spending Christmas with me at my sister's. You don't expect me to keep my hands to myself, do you?"

A slow, seductive grin played across her face. "You better not. I like your hands on me."

He kissed her again, softly, slowly, so filled with tenderness her heart ached to tell him she loved him.

"James, do you want—oh."

They both flinched, snapping their direction to Theresa.

A light shade of red rushed across Theresa's face. "I didn't mean to...you know...interrupt." Another sappy smile emerged. "It's nice to see you two together. It makes me very happy."

James stiffened, yet an easygoing smile stayed on his face. What was that about? He just said he didn't care who knew. Maybe he really did care? Why did the tension return?

"Did you need something, Tessie?"

The question came out normal, no hint of disgust, aggravation, or annoyance. Yet James still felt stiff. Like an invisible shield had sprung up as soon as Theresa said she was happy to see them together.

"Jelly on your toast? I know you like jelly. Did you want grape or strawberry?" Theresa looked at her. "And I need to know what you like as well, Erin."

"Butter is fine. Thank you, Theresa." She moved her hand around under the blanket until she found James' hand, then gripped it hard, offering some comfort, even though she didn't know why she had to.

"Grape. Thanks," James replied.

Theresa's brows furrowed for a brief moment, then the dose of concern diminished and her happy, vibrant smile was back in place. "It shouldn't be too much longer. You guys are welcome to stay for a while if you want, or Aiden can take you home as soon as you finish eating. It's up to you."

James only nodded but didn't answer with a specific response. As soon as Theresa walked out of the room, she took her free hand out from under the blanket and touched his cheek, turning his head to look her dead in the eye. She was going to start meeting any issue head-on with him. She wouldn't let him keep running from her, from talking things out.

"What was that?"

He frowned, feigning ignorance. "What?"

"One minute you're telling me you don't care who knows, including your sister, that you want me to come over for Christmas, and the next minute you're tensing up when she says how nice it is and how happy she is to see us together. Which one is it? Which one is the truth, James? You want people to know, or you don't?"

"I do. I don't care who knows." His eyes looked down, even though her hand held his cheek, refusing to let him turn away from her. "But I'm still leaving town. It kills me to—"

Her hand brushed across his cheek to his mouth, stopping him. She held her hand over his mouth, debating. Should she confess she had been thinking about leaving with him? Not simply quitting her job and finding a new one in town, but packing all her belongings and going wherever he ventured off to. She had a long, cold night wrapped in his sweet, gentle arms to think about it. And she knew what she wanted.

The question was, how would James take it? Would he smile and be excited at the prospect? Or shove her away, thinking it was for her own good?

Or worse, tell her he wasn't that into her. It was only sex. Friends with benefits.

She could confess she loved him first, then dive into the fact that she was leaving with him whether he liked it or not.

Of course, this wasn't the ideal time to have this kind of conversation, with his sister in the kitchen making them breakfast, his brother-in-law outside, and the chance to walk in at any time.

"I know you're leaving."

His eyes glanced up.

"I'm not going to talk you out of it." She smiled, hoping to ease the worry and concern in his tortured gaze.

"I didn't think you would."

"So, what's the problem?" She couldn't confess her true feelings yet. Not until they were alone, with no possible interruptions to ruin a serious conversation.

His hand came out from under the blanket, placing it over hers on his cheek. A tender smile split across his face. "I want you. I want you in my arms. I don't care who knows as long as you're happy. But I also don't want to hurt you, Erin. When my sister says we look happy and it's nice to see us together, it cements it even further into my heart that I'm going to hurt you when I leave."

Pressing her lips gently to his, she wanted to bite him instead. The kiss would have to suffice for the moment. "Let me worry about my hurt feelings. I'm a big girl, James."

Plus, she was planning on going with him. No hurt feelings.

"I wish I could stay, Erin. I wish I could give you everything you deserve." His hand grasped hers, pulling it to his lap, squeezing with a desperation she hated feeling. "I don't want to leave you. But it's something I have to do. I can't stay here anymore."

"What the hell are you talking about? Leaving?"

This time they didn't flinch, they jumped from the angry voice of Aiden, who had walked into the living room unnoticed.

"Well? Please explain. Are you talking about leaving this

house? Or leaving..." Aiden's voice trailed off as he glanced toward the kitchen, where soft sounds could be heard from Theresa. His gaze connected with James, hard and unyielding. "Tell me the truth so I can prepare my wife for the worst."

James went rigid again with tension, then he unwrapped his arm from around her and stood up. "I'm done with this dumbass town. I'm *leaving* leaving. Theresa will be fine."

Aiden rubbed a hand down his face. "But will you be? With no support around you? I know we don't always get along, James, but you're my family, whether you like it or not. I hate to see you go down...the wrong road."

His hands tightened into fists. Erin wanted to stand up, smooth one of his fists out and offer her support. But she didn't know how James would react—if he would want her doing that in front of Aiden.

"I don't have any damn support here."

Aiden moved forward two steps, nearly shouting, "You have me and Theresa. You have Terry. You have a lot more people than you realize."

James' hands relaxed as soon as he saw Theresa step into the room, her brows pleated with concern.

"What are you two arguing about?" Theresa asked, looking at everyone in the room, even her as if she might give some insight into the situation.

And she could. She understood perfectly why James wanted to leave. He had every right to feel that way. They didn't know he wouldn't be alone when he left. Hell, James didn't even know he wouldn't be alone. Because she was going with.

Aiden took ahold of Theresa's hand as she stepped closer to him. He looked like he wanted to say something, but then glanced at James and nothing but silence continued to fill the room. Even James kept looking back and forth between Aiden and Theresa but didn't say a word.

Erin finally stood up and grabbed James' hand in a tight grip, the same as Aiden held Theresa's hand.

"James is moving. He hasn't decided where yet. But he's leaving town because it's the best thing for him." Erin didn't look James' way to see if he was upset with her, but she didn't need to. She knew he wasn't angry when he squeezed her hand.

"They can't fire you, James. And you can't leave without fighting it," Theresa said softly, but with so much conviction it made Erin smile.

She was so glad Theresa believed in her brother. James needed that.

"I'm done fighting with this town, Tessie."

Erin hated the despair laced in his tone as he responded.

Theresa's eyes narrowed, completely different from the smiles she had been doling out minutes before. "Well, Aiden isn't. Neither am I. He called Chief Duncan, who's looking into the issue, probably as we speak."

If Erin thought he was filled with tension before, his body snapped taut with anger and so much rage she was afraid to let go of his hand to see how he might react.

"What the hell are you talking about, he went to Chief Duncan?"

Aiden frowned. "You seem mighty upset about that, James? Why?"

"Because you're messing in my business and I don't like it, *Officer Crowl*," James spat.

Aiden let go of Theresa's hand and took a step forward. "Or because you actually did steal those prescription drugs."

Erin clutched James' hand so hard she felt like she could break it. Because the fury flowing through his veins was easy to detect. One wrong move and he was going to let go and plow a fist right into Aiden.

Hell, she wanted to herself for Aiden questioning James. So she would.

She gripped his hand a little harder, then abruptly let go and stepped into Aiden's face, poking him in the chest.

Okay, she didn't believe in violence, but he'd still see her wrath.

"Take it back. Right now."

In a childish way, apparently. Whatever worked.

NOTHING about this situation was funny. Not one word.

And yet James wanted to grin from ear to ear and break out in laughter at Erin's sweet, adorable words. *Take it back. Right now.* As if they were on the playground having a beef with the mean kids at school.

She poked Aiden again, not satisfied with his silence. James was tempted to step forward, push her out of the way, and lay a fist into his face. Which was probably what Erin knew he wanted to do and decided to take control of the situation. If Aiden put his hands on her for any reason, James would move so fast he wouldn't see the punch coming. But for now, he'd stay behind her, letting her play his hero. He liked it. No one had ever stood up for him like this.

Honestly, he was a little too shocked to do anything but watch as the situation played out.

God, he loved this woman.

He wanted to tell her. Right here and now. While she

was poking his brother-in-law in the chest, demanding he take his words back.

The fight in Aiden died as his shoulders drooped and his body relaxed. He took a step back toward Theresa as he looked him straight in the eye. "I'm sorry. I keep forgetting how hardheaded you can be. How you hate help even when you need it sometimes. I was just trying to help you." Aiden's mouth formed a thin line. "I *am* trying to help you. Whether you want it or not."

"I definitely don't want it," he all but growled, low and menacing. Damn it, he didn't want anything from Aiden or his sister. Didn't they see how that might drag them down, too? That's the last thing he wanted.

"Tough." Aiden jerked when Theresa slid her hand into his.

"Call him and tell him to let it go. This isn't just about me." James threw a hand in Theresa's direction. "I don't need people smearing my sister's name because of me."

A gentle smile emerged on Aiden's face as he raised Theresa's hand locked in his and kissed the back of it. "Your sister is stronger than she looks. Nobody will smear her name if I have anything to say about it."

The urge to have a drink attacked him. A strong, stiff drink to wash away these erratic emotions coursing through him. Anger, rage, worry, concern, a little bit of awe that Aiden would help him in any way.

"James, maybe you don't see it, but I'm a cop and I do." Aiden's expression looked serious, filled with brotherly concern. "You didn't steal those drugs." He looked at Erin, nodding as if telling her he firmly believed that. Erin nodded back, then Aiden looked at James. "But someone stole those drugs and is trying to place the blame on you. That's not okay."

"I don't—"

Erin turned around and placed a hand on his chest, stopping him. Her soft touch made some of the fight disappear. She calmed him down when a lot of the time he felt like he was fighting a daily war with himself. Just one light touch simmered his emotions enough to think clearly.

"Chief Duncan is a smart man. He will find the truth," Erin whispered.

After hearing Erin's soft words, he agreed. Chief Duncan would find the truth. Maybe to keep the townsfolk from smearing his sister's name, he had to stand back and let Chief Duncan do his job. When he left, he wanted only good things said about her. He wouldn't be able to stand it if they talked about her because of him behind her back.

"I'm still leaving, even with the truth out," he said quietly, speaking only to Erin, although his sister heard by the sharp intake of her breath.

Erin stepped closer, her hand still pressed strongly to his chest. "I won't stop you from leaving. I support your decision."

Clutching her hand against his chest, he raised it to his mouth. "I don't deserve you. But I'm—" *Not letting you get away* wanted to break free.

But he couldn't say that because that implied he wanted her to come with him. He could never ask Erin to pick up her life and go wherever he decided to go.

She took another step closer. "You're what? Finish that sentence."

He couldn't. No matter how true it felt inside. No matter how much he loved her. He couldn't drag her with him. She'd eventually resent him. Hate him for making her leave.

He kissed her instead of answering. When he backed away, she grinned deviously. "This conversation is far from over, James. You're still running from me, and you didn't even move one step."

Damn, but she read him well. He was running. He'd run as far away from her as he could.

She was better off without him in her life.

15

AFTER A TENSE BREAKFAST, emotions still running high, Aiden said he'd take them home. She hadn't been ready to leave James yet, but for now, it was for the best.

Erin closed the door, fighting the urge to go back outside, stop James from leaving, and demand he stay with her while she put her affairs in order. But then he'd want to argue with her about quitting her job, so it was better he left.

A sharp pang hit her heart. She rubbed a hand over her chest as she tried to block out scenarios of how the conversation was going between James and Aiden. Would they get into an argument?

Well, thinking about it wouldn't change anything. If they did, they did. She'd give Aiden a piece of her mind later if he said anything to upset James.

Throwing her small duffle bag she had at the cabin on the washing machine to wash later, she headed for the shower. She took her time under the hot, soothing water, especially after sleeping all night and walking for as long as they had in the freezing weather. When the water started to cool, she knew it was time to get out.

She pulled out a pair of jeans and a nice thick sweater, one of her favorite Christmas sweaters. Two years ago at the hospital Christmas party, she won the best Ugly Christmas Sweater contest. Her sweater was dark blue with a large Christmas tree. Sitting in the branches were faces of little cats peeking out. Sprawled across the top and the bottom of the tree were the words "Meowy Catmas." The lights on the tree lit up, flashing bright colors while a hilarious song played "We wish you a meowy catmas" with holiday cheer. She was proud of that win. She even received an award certificate. Some might find it silly, but she was proud of winning. She didn't win much in her life.

It was a little over the top, especially since she wasn't going to a party, but it made her smile. That's what she needed right now. She needed to smile.

She was going to quit her job.

She grabbed her purse from where she had stuffed it in the duffle bag and searched for her car keys.

Then it dawned on her.

She had no way to get to the hospital. Or anywhere. Her car was stuck out in the middle of nowhere, near the cabin she wanted to go back to. She wanted to snuggle with James and forget about the real world until she had no choice but to face her problems head-on.

Because the hospital wasn't the only problem she had to face. She'd have to see her uncle and tell him she was leaving. It shouldn't be a big deal, considering she didn't visit as often as she had in the beginning, but she tried to visit at least three times a week. He was used to seeing her around, getting his little digs in here and there whenever the opportunity presented itself, which was all the time because he didn't know how to hold his tongue—and because he didn't care who he hurt.

She'd miss her aunt, but it was time to move on. They didn't need her help anymore. Her aunt had a full-time nurse to take care of her, even though Erin thought she'd do much better in a facility with more professionals around.

But her uncle had all the say. Not her.

Putting on her jacket, hat, mittens, and scarf, she decided she could handle walking a few blocks to the hospital. Clear her mind of her worries for a while. It was a good thing she didn't live too far away.

Making her way down the sidewalk, enjoying the warm sun beating down, although the chills still attacked her from the cold bite in the air, she knew she was making the right decision.

Hopefully James thought the same thing when she told him it was official. He'd probably be upset, thinking she was ruining her life for a loser.

He was no loser.

He was a kind, sweet guy. People simply didn't look beneath the surface to see it.

She made it to the hospital without any toes or fingers falling off, and with the way the cold wrapped around her, invading her skin, she could imagine it happening. Maybe walking hadn't been the best idea.

Waving hello to Tonya behind the counter—a place she sat every day, a place she wouldn't miss—the more the idea cemented in her mind that she was making the right decision. She headed straight for Dr. Pearson's office. She unzipped her coat, her bright colorful Christmas sweater on display. A few people smiled and waved as she passed by.

Rounding the corner, she halted in her steps when she saw Chief Duncan outside Dr. Pearson's office, anger displayed in every facet of his body. Dr. Pearson didn't look very happy either. Their voices weren't loud, but she could tell by their postures and pinched expressions that it wasn't a pleasant conversation.

Dr. Pearson saw her first. Then Chief Duncan turned his attention her way. She found the strength to move, although typically she'd offer a smile or a pleasant gesture. Not today. Not now.

"Hi, Erin. How are you?" Chief Duncan said, his brows pleated, yet trying to attempt a smile. Then a real smile lit his features when he looked at her sweater. She had turned on the lights, so the tree was lit up in all its glorious silliness, blinking and singing its cute cat tune. "I love the sweater."

"Thank you. I needed something to cheer me up. It hasn't been a great day." She turned her full attention to Dr. Pearson. "It could be much better if some people weren't treated so callously."

Dr. Pearson's jaw clenched, his brows furrowed low. "I've had about enough of people accusing me of treating some people wrong."

"He didn't do it."

"I have a witness who said he did." Dr. Pearson relaxed his features, looking almost bored with the conversation.

"And I would like to know who this witness is," Chief Duncan demanded, not an ounce of politeness in his tone.

"I'm not pressing charges, so it's not any of your concern."

Chief Duncan leaned closer to Dr. Pearson. "Anything that goes on in this town is my concern. Especially if someone is stealing drugs." He backed away. "And I don't think that someone is James."

Erin wanted to smile at Chief Duncan's firm tone when

he said he believed in James' innocence. She didn't smile, though. Right now wasn't the time or place for smiles.

"Look, I don't care what you think, Chief. I didn't ask you to come here and interrogate me, especially when I've done nothing wrong. I have a witness. I did what I had to do and the matter is settled." Dr. Pearson nodded as if his word was gold.

"The matter is far from settled. You fired an innocent man." Erin pinned him with an evil stare, fully ready to quit after hearing him sound so stoic about James. "The fact that you don't want to give up your witness tells me you're hiding something. Sure, James has a shady past, so, of course he makes a good fall man. Nobody's going to care that he got fired. Well, news flash," she shouted, "I care. I quit. I refuse to work where they treat their employees with no remorse."

Dr. Pearson's expression fell into sorrow. A bit surprising, considering his nonchalance from moments before. "Erin, let's talk about this. Chief Duncan's leaving. Come into my office so we can talk."

He took a step back, holding out his arm for her to proceed him.

She responded with a quick shake of her head. "We have nothing to speak about. Unless you plan to tell me who your supposed witness is."

"I have to agree with Erin," Chief Duncan said. "I've always respected you, Dr. Pearson. Today, I've lost a tremendous amount of that respect. If you have nothing to hide, you wouldn't mind telling me, the chief of police," his expression changed into pain, "and your friend."

The silence stretched. The seconds ticked down as she and Chief Duncan didn't waver their stern glare in Dr. Pearson's direction. The longer they stared, the more he started to fidget. First, his hands, twitching slightly. Then, his feet, moving around a bit.

Dr. Pearson's mouth opened, then closed. He glanced up and down the hallway, then stepped into his office, waving his hand. "Fine. Come in and I'll tell you everything I know."

Chief Duncan gave her a delicate smile and then held out his hand for her to go first. She was very grateful to have him with her. Not simply because he was the chief of police and he could arrest Dr. Pearson if need be, but Chief Duncan always made her feel safe. And right now, she didn't feel safe, especially with the way Dr. Pearson had looked up and down the hallway.

She took a seat in front of his desk. Chief Duncan sat next to her in the other chair, as Dr. Pearson sat behind his desk.

Before he said a word, she popped up her hand like she was in a classroom looking for permission to speak. Dr. Pearson nodded.

"I want you to know before you say anything, it doesn't matter what you tell us. I quit. I'm leaving Mulberry altogether."

JAMES TRIED to shut the door in Aiden's face, but his hand against the door prevented it. Aiden's determined expression said he'd have to throw a few punches to get his way. The last thing he needed to do was punch his sister's husband and have to explain why he did such a thing.

Rolling his eyes, he left the door alone, tossed his duffle bag to the floor, and took off his jacket and slung it across the couch. He didn't wait for Aiden to start speaking, or whatever the hell he planned to do since he forced his way into his home. He headed for the kitchen for a drink. Any drink. Water. Coffee. Juice. He couldn't have alcohol because he didn't have any in the house, but damn, he could use a glass of something strong.

He didn't know why Aiden decided now was a good time to have a chat. They had the entire car ride to speak. Except neither said a word. Only the light Christmas music playing had filled the car. Aiden didn't seem like the kind of person who listened to Christmas music. He figured his sister had to have been listening to it last and Aiden chose to keep it on. To remind him that he shouldn't leave his sister.

It's not like he wanted to leave his sister. He didn't want to leave Terry either.

But he also didn't want to stay. He was ready for a change. To find a new kind of happiness somewhere else. Because here, in this dumb small town, happiness was rare.

The only time he felt a bit of happiness was when he was talking to Erin at work, or spending time with his sister.

He wanted to move somewhere where people didn't know his history unless he wanted to tell them about his past. He didn't want to keep being judged on his character for his past transgressions. Was that too much to ask? For people to judge him for the man he was now, not before.

Pulling a glass from the cupboard, he slammed it on the counter. It didn't break, and for a brief second, he wished it had. He had so much anger, resentment, and pain warping him inside, he needed to release it somehow. Breaking things sounded like the perfect start.

Or punching something.

Aiden, for example.

Or, so he didn't upset his sister, he could take up boxing or something. That might be therapeutic.

"Can we talk, James?"

With his hand still curled around the glass, he thought about slamming it against the counter again or squeezing until it crushed in his hand.

"I'm not trying to upset you or anything. I want to talk."

Nothing Aiden said would change his mind, but if talking would get him out of his house faster, fine. He'd talk. He let out a slow breath, released the glass from his tight grip, and turned around.

"What?"

Aiden had his hands in his jacket pockets. To help hold him back because he wanted to punch him, too? The idea almost made him laugh.

"We haven't always gotten along, or liked each other." Aiden grinned as if to lessen the blow of the truth he already knew. "I'd do anything for Theresa. I love her so much." His eyes turned to the floor. "Over the past few years, even though we've had some rough patches, I've come to the realization that I'd do anything for you, too."

"Yeah, for my sister. I got it." He didn't know what that proved. It's not anything new he had heard from Aiden.

Aiden's gaze slowly raised. "No. For you. Because I think of you as my brother. You've been through some tough stuff, and being right by your side as you dealt with it..." He shrugged. "Well, it's brought us closer. I'd like to think I helped you through some of those hard times, not just Theresa."

James looked away this time, unsure of how to respond. Yeah, Aiden had been through some of those harder days, especially the first few months when he really struggled for a drink. When he ached so badly for one little taste he thought he'd never survive. Some nights, Aiden would stop by after his shift, play a video game with him, then head home to Theresa. They didn't say much to each other. Nothing too personal, anyway.

But yeah, as he thought about it, those times had helped him. They centered him. Made him not ache for a drink.

Why didn't he see that before?

Why didn't he see how much Aiden had helped him?

Maybe because he still wanted to hate the guy for being so perfect. Life was always easy for him. He didn't know the meaning of struggle.

Turning his attention back to Aiden, ready to dismiss his words with the sharp sting of his tongue, the words stalled. The ache, the pain hidden in the depths of Aiden's eyes stopped him.

How could he forget? Aiden wasn't perfect. Nor was his life. His former fiancé died in a car crash. That couldn't have been easy to deal with.

Everyone had struggles. Sometimes James forgot, only thinking of himself. Was he being selfish wanting to leave town?

"Yeah, okay."

Aiden's brow rose skeptically. "Yeah, okay, what?"

A tiny chuckle emerged as a grin grew. "Maybe I appreciated your help a little bit." James tossed a shoulder up casually as if he didn't care. "If I did, by chance, think of you as a brother, it'd be an annoying younger brother that pisses me off too much."

Aiden laughed. "Well, don't get me wrong, I think of you as an older brother that pisses me off and never listens to the wisdom I have."

He scoffed, then laughter filled the air. "Wisdom, huh? Since when are you full of wisdom?"

The smile on Aiden's face widened. "I have my moments."

James cleared his throat, wanting this heart-to-heart to be finished, but oddly enough, he wasn't craving a drink as badly anymore.

"Now that we have that out of the way, can I speak freely?"

James crossed his arms, chuckling. "Wow, that wasn't you speaking freely? Could've fooled me."

Laughter echoed back. Aiden's face lit up with pleasure. "I feel like we're making ground here and I hate to ruin it." The smile stayed firm, but the hesitancy was in his eyes. "It's selfish—"

"Get the hell out." He stood up ramrod straight, his arms falling to his sides, his hands fisting into tight balls. Yeah, Aiden should've stopped while he was ahead. He ruined the damn moment.

Aiden held up his hands. "You could let me finish. It's not what you think." He lowered his hands when James did nothing but stand there, staring at him violently. "I was trying to say it's selfish of me to ask you to stay just for Theresa. I know she'll miss you," his lips curled into a grin, "and so will I, strange as it might seem. But I know this is something you have to do. What I'm trying to say is I fully support you. Whatever you need, I'm here to help. If you need help packing, moving your stuff, finding a place to stay, a job, whatever it is, I'm here."

All the anger and rage that had built instantly deflated like a balloon losing its air. His fists loosened as his shoulders drooped.

"I get wanting to disappear. I get the feeling like nothing in your world makes sense and you have to find that one thing to center it." Aiden smiled, his eyes filling up with pleasure. "Theresa centers me. I would still be lost in a deep fog, going through the motions of life like a robot, if it wasn't for her. If moving, if leaving town, is what you need, then of course I fully support it. I wasn't thinking clearly when I first heard it. But now that I've had time to think, I understand why. Theresa will understand. I know she will."

They stared at each other, obviously Aiden waiting for him to say something. Except he didn't know what to say. Too many emotions were crowding him, screaming at him in all directions.

"I don't regret going to Chief Duncan. I did that, not to hurt you, but to help you. It's not right, James, what the hospital did. I won't stand around letting people hurt you."

"Thank you."

It was the only thing that came forth that seemed appropriate.

"I wish I knew what centered me like Theresa does for you." James shrugged, shuffling his feet as he looked at the floor. "I'm hoping when I leave, I'll find that thing."

"Are you sure you haven't found it?"

He met Aiden's eyes. "What?"

"Erin. With the way you were staring at her today, I figured she was the one that centered you."

16

ERIN DECIDED to sit back and let Chief Duncan handle this. After her announcement that she was still quitting regardless of what Dr. Pearson said, the room had been silent. She didn't think she'd render people speechless with her choice to leave. Maybe it was more because she was leaving due to defending James, a person people didn't think deserved that kind of defending.

"Your witness, Dr. Pearson. You can share any time," Chief Duncan said, casually, as if they were all sitting around for a nice chat about the weather.

"What will you do with this information?" Dr. Pearson shifted in his chair, clearly uncomfortable that he decided to share. Hopefully, anyway. The way he kept moving around, twitching with nervousness, said he might change his mind.

Chief Duncan's eyes narrowed. "It shouldn't matter. Do you want the fact that you fired an innocent man on your conscience?"

Dr. Pearson folded his hands, laying them on top of his desk. "I have a witness that says he did it."

"A witness you refuse to tell me about."

"Fine," Dr. Pearson muttered, his hands clasping tighter together. "Dr. Colton said he saw James leaving the pharmacy when it should've been closed. After checking the records, we noticed that some drugs disappeared over the past four months. A little here, a little there."

A brow rose as Erin tried hard not to shout vile things at a man she used to respect. "That's it? He saw him leaving the pharmacy. He *is* the janitor. He was probably cleaning things up, changing the garbage cans. Did he see him with any drugs?"

"Once the pharmacy is closed, no one, not even the janitor, goes in there. He should be cleaning during business hours." Dr. Pearson shifted again in his chair, looking at his clasped hands. "He didn't actually see any drugs in his hands."

Chief Duncan cleared his throat. "You fired a man over that. Because he was seen leaving the pharmacy after hours?"

Dr. Pearson looked up, meeting Chief Duncan's stern gaze. "Dr. Colton is a good doctor. I can't afford to lose him right now."

"What does that even mean? Why would you lose him?"

His hands shook, gripped together, yet Dr. Pearson didn't look away. "I wasn't completely sure I believed him about James, but James…"

"Just because he had an alcohol problem doesn't mean he has a drug problem. Talk about judgmental," Erin spat, even more disgusted with a man she never thought she'd hate.

"I'm not proud of it, but the fact remains, drugs are missing," Dr. Pearson inhaled deeply, keeping his stance that James did it even though he had a bit of doubt.

"Do you think Dr. Colton took the drugs? Is that why

you were worried about losing him?" Chief Duncan asked with a tone that said he better not ignore him.

"Of course not," Dr. Pearson said with disbelief. "I didn't want to lose him for lying, and honestly, I'm not sure why he'd lie that he saw James leaving the pharmacy."

Chief Duncan stood up. "I'd like to speak with Dr. Colton."

"Absolutely not. There's no need. This is not a police issue," Dr. Pearson exclaimed, standing up himself.

Erin stayed in her seat, watching, glancing between the two as they stared hard and unyieldingly at each other.

"You have missing drugs. Something like that is definitely a police issue. I'm making it my issue. And it's something you should've reported immediately. It almost makes me wonder whether you took the drugs yourself," Chief Duncan said it quietly as if it pained him to speak.

Dr. Pearson's mouth opened and closed, his expression wavering into remorse. "I should've reported it. Without Dr. Colton telling us anything, it might've gone unreported for a while. Why would he lie?"

Chief Duncan sighed. "Why does anyone lie, Dr. Pearson? Because they don't want to get caught. You should've, as it's your duty, reported this to the DEA, if not me. You can't fire a man and brush it under the rug and say it's been taken care of. You have drugs that went missing. A crime was committed. If it happened to be James, then that's something he needs to answer to. If it happens to be someone else, lying about James to cover their own ass, then they need to answer to it. As the chief of police, it's my job to uphold the law. I'm doing my job whether you like it or not. Why don't you do *your* job?"

Dr. Pearson swallowed hard, then sat down. A deep breath released as his expression morphed into worry. "Of course, Chief Duncan. You're right. I will do what I should've done immediately."

Nodding, his expression neutral, Chief Duncan then turned to her. "We're done here, Erin. Shall we?"

She stood up, not even bothering to look at Dr. Pearson.

"Is Dr. Colton working right now?" Chief Duncan asked as she headed for the hallway to escape the tension swirling around the small office.

"He is. You can find him on the fifth floor," Dr. Pearson said without emotion. "I don't know what happened. How this all spiraled so out of control."

"It started when you fired a man based on very little evidence." Chief Duncan then followed her, guiding her out of the office with a light hand to her back. "Are you okay, Erin?"

"I'm fine."

He smiled tenderly. "That was intense. Are you sure you're okay? It's always disappointing when someone you know and respect breaks the trust you had in them. I can't believe he'd go this far and deal with this situation the way he did."

She returned his smile with one of her own. Oh, she knew all about breaking trust firsthand with her uncle. "I have this feeling before the day is over, you're going to get to the bottom of it, aren't you?"

"It's my job." The smile on his face said he was very proud of his job and his ability to do it as well as he did.

Erin had all the faith in the world he'd find the truth.

"Keep me updated? For James' sake," she asked with the hope tinged in her voice.

"I didn't know you two were so close." The question in his tone said he wanted to know more. "But I will tell you the outcome. Merry Christmas, Erin. I hope you both have a great Christmas despite what's going on."

"Thank you, Chief Duncan. I have a feeling it's going to be wonderful. I won't let this ruin anything."

And she wouldn't. She might have her work cut out for her to get James to enjoy it, keep him from worrying about everything, but she liked challenges now and again.

She said goodbye to Chief Duncan and made her way out of the hospital and into the cold once more.

As soon as she got home, she'd see about getting her car freed from the snow, if it was even possible yet, then do a little Christmas shopping. She needed to get James a present.

She also needed to see her uncle.

That was not going to be a pleasant conversation.

"ARE we done here with our little heart-to-heart?" James asked with a laugh, trying to hide the fact of how much Aiden's support in his decision meant. He was shocked, to say the least.

Aiden chuckled, the merry sound filling the tiny kitchen. "Yeah, I'm tapped out with sentiment for the day."

"Thanks for the ride home." He slumped against the counter. "It'd be nice to have my car, though. I'm sure Erin needs hers as well."

"Well, the roads seem to be getting better. We could take Bentley's truck back out there. He has a plow on the front of his truck."

"That'd be great."

Aiden nodded and pulled out his phone, walking away to call Bentley. James grabbed the pitcher of water from the fridge and poured some into the glass waiting patiently for him on the counter. He downed the contents in one swallow. It was so refreshing, the icy cold water sliding down his throat, almost soothing, that he poured another glass and downed that one just as fast.

He put the pitcher of water back in the fridge and his cup in the sink.

Once he got his car unstuck, he'd have to go to the grocery store. He didn't have much to talk about food-wise in his house, especially if he planned to make Erin something special tonight.

She was still coming over tonight, right?

Would time away from him change her mind?

God, he hoped not.

Well, worrying about it wouldn't change the outcome. He had learned that lesson a long time ago.

After grabbing some groceries, he'd find Erin a Christmas present. She said she was spending Christmas with him and he'd hold her to it. By bribing her with a present.

Ha, bribing!

Did he have to do that?

She said she wanted to spend the day with him and his family, so he had to believe her.

"James!"

Whirling around from the sink, he cocked a brow at Aiden, hiding the fact that he caught him off guard. "Why are you yelling at me? I thought we were past that."

A slow smirk emerged. "I said your name like five times before I yelled. Is someone special on your mind?"

James rolled his eyes and walked away from the sink. He was not going to talk to Aiden about his feelings for Erin. "Are we getting my car or what?"

"Yeah, Bentley will come with. We're going to meet him out there."

They left right away. Bentley was already there by the time they arrived, plowing around the vehicles. Within the hour, they had his and Erin's cars freed from the snow. Bentley's truck had managed to plow around both vehicles without moving either one since they didn't think to grab Erin's car keys from her first. With a bit of maneuvering, James was able to drive around Erin's car and get back on the main road.

"Well, we have one too many vehicles now and not enough people." Bentley chuckled as he looked at the cars and truck lining the road.

"You can head out, Bentley. Thanks for the help. James can follow me home in his car so we can drop mine off. Then we'll come back for Erin's. I'll bring Erin her car."

An immediate frown punctured his face, his brows burrowing low as jealousy filled his veins. "Why do *you* have to drop her car off?"

Aiden slapped him on the shoulder playfully as his laughter rang through the air. "You told me you were making her dinner on the ride here. Don't you need to get ready for that? I'll drop her car off, she can give me a ride home, and then she can make her way to you. That should give you plenty of time to grab some groceries and get home to cook."

Some of the jealousy dissipated as what Aiden said started to sink in. It all made sense.

It was Erin's fault he let it get to him. She just had to confess she had a crush on Aiden at one time. Whenever he thought about them together, it sent his jealousy skyrocketing to deadly levels. The golden boy. She had to have a crush on the damn golden boy.

Aiden squeezed his shoulder, his expression softening into concern. "James, I'm happily married to your sister. That angry look on your face doesn't need to be there."

He blew out a breath and stepped back. Aiden's hand fell away. "I know. And if you hurt my sister, I hurt you."

"Got it." Aiden winked, chuckling. Probably to loosen the tension swirling around with the brisk, cold wind.

It helped. Somewhat.

He hated thinking about those two together, even talking in a friendly manner.

Trying to forget about it, he tossed his head at Bentley. "Thanks for the help. I appreciate it."

"Anytime. Stay warm." Bentley waved goodbye and hopped into his truck.

James and Aiden headed for Aiden's house to drop off his car. Aiden exited his vehicle and tapped on his window. Rolling it down, James shivered from the cold air rushing inside his warm haven.

Aiden grinned crookedly. It immediately pissed him off for some reason. Then Aiden spoke and he knew why.

"I don't have Erin's car keys. I'll have to drive over to her house first and then take her to her car."

"Fine." He knew his one-worded answer sounded clipped, but he didn't care.

"You can do it, buddy." Aiden shrugged, the damn grin still on his face. "I'm trying to help you." His grin slowly melted away. "You like her, don't you?"

James' hands gripped the steering wheel. "Yes."

"Then woo her. Make it special. I'm giving you some time to do that."

Glancing away, looking out the window, the tension and impulsive anger gradually disappeared as he took a few deep breaths. He looked back at Aiden. "It's not you.

Honestly," he said with a chuckle, thinking back to Erin's confession. "It has nothing to do with you. Call it insecurity."

"Dude, we all have it. Women make us men crazy. It's their job."

James laughed, the sweet sound making him feel good. He hadn't laughed this much in a very long time. It felt so, so good. "Thanks for the help. I forgot to mention, but Erin's my guest for Christmas. Can you fit her in the menu? Tell Theresa sorry for the late notice."

"It's all good. I'm glad she's coming with you." Aiden's brows puckered low. "So, you're leaving town...what about Erin?"

James inhaled and exhaled deeply, hating the question. But it was a damn good question.

"I haven't thought that far ahead yet. Thanks again, man."

He rolled up his window before Aiden could interrogate him more. He had enough dissecting his feelings about everything.

He had work to do.

Time to impress the woman he loved.

Maybe he should tell her.

Maybe she'd think about coming with him.

Yeah, maybe she would. But he couldn't do it. That'd be selfish. And he'd never be selfish with Erin.

17

Erin squared her shoulders, blew out a small breath, and knocked on the door. By the time she got home and made a few phone calls, she was surprised to find Aiden would be dropping by so she could pick up her vehicle. After tidying up her house, making a grocery list, and thinking of a good Christmas present for James, Aiden showed up. Not long after that, they drove to her vehicle and he made sure she didn't get stuck backing out before he left.

Once she arrived home, she set about her tasks she wanted to complete before the day ended. She figured starting with the most difficult task would be best.

Which brought her waiting in front of a door she hoped wouldn't open.

Her hopes were dashed when the door swung open to a stern man. In the five years she had been in Mulberry to help him, she had never seen a genuine smile.

"Erin, what a surprise. Come on in."

She smiled at her uncle and stepped inside, the warmth immediately filling her up. When she connected her gaze with his, a slight chill passed through her. She hated thinking of him as a cruel man. He had some nice qualities. But when his sharp tongue badgered a person over and over, it was hard to remember what those nice qualities were.

"Hi, Uncle Martin. I was—"

"Shouldn't you be at work? Especially after such a snowstorm." His brows puckered into a disapproving frown, unaffected that he cut her off so rudely. "Of course, you're not an actual nurse, so maybe they don't need you."

There it was. Little dig here. Little dig there. Never once did he apologize for the things he said.

"I have off through Christmas."

He tsked, shaking his head as if she said something so ludicrous. "All play and no work does not pay the bills."

He walked away, expecting her to follow, which she did after removing her shoes. She decided to keep her jacket on, although stuffed her hat, scarf, and mittens in her jacket pockets. She didn't plan to stay too long. She could only handle her uncle in low doses these days.

He hadn't been so bad in the beginning when she first moved to town, showing up every day to help with her aunt. But as time went on, as her aunt's health started to deteriorate more, his demeanor and behavior worsened as well. At first, she thought he was dealing with the pain of losing his wife to such a horrible disease in the only way he knew how. Then she saw him smirk after delivering a brutal cutdown that almost made her cry. He did it because he enjoyed it.

"We missed you yesterday. You didn't call and tell me you wouldn't be coming," he said as he stopped at the kitchen counter.

She tried to keep the smile on her face. Stuck in the middle of the cabin, enjoying the time with James, she forgot she usually visited them on Thursdays. Although she had no reception so it wouldn't have mattered if she called or not. Plus, there had been a nasty snowstorm. What did he expect?

"I'm sorry, Uncle Martin. I was snowed in with a friend and I didn't have any reception. I'm here today."

"Hmmm." He didn't say anything else as he poured himself some coffee but didn't offer her any.

"How's Aunt Maura?" That's all she cared to know at this point.

"Resting. I read her a book earlier. Something you should've done yesterday." The disapproval was back in his features as he took a sip of coffee.

She could repeat what she previously said or completely ignore his dig.

"I'd like to say hi to her."

"I don't believe you have a hearing problem, Erin. She's resting."

She could fight him. Maybe say a few nasty words herself. Or she could let it go and come to terms with the fact that she wouldn't be able to see her aunt today. She'd try again before she moved away.

Because, oh, she was moving away from this hell. From this asshole.

Her sister had been right. Even without being near their uncle and dealing with him day in and day out as she had, her sister had known he would be like this.

Taking her hat out of her pocket, she placed it on her head, her smile still displayed like bright, brilliant lights on a Christmas tree. Although, it was completely fake. "Well, I'll leave you be. I wanted to stop by and see Aunt Maura." She smiled even wider. "And to say I'll be moving soon."

A muscle ticked in his jaw, the only indication that he was affected by her news. And for him, that was quite a sign of surprise. "Moving where?"

She shrugged, laughing joyfully, knowing he'd hate her answer. "I was thinking of pulling out a map, closing my eyes, and going wherever my finger lands. Sounds fun, right?"

"Sounds irresponsible. You should know better, Erin."

"I hope you have a merry Christmas, Uncle Martin. Unfortunately, I thought I'd be able to make it this year, but I can't."

He took another sip of his coffee, then set the mug down on the counter as if he were about to cut the wire on a bomb. "I went to the store today. I heard some disturbing news."

Oh, she could imagine what he heard.

"That alcoholic is only going to bring you trouble. Look at you already. Quitting your job. Moving away. Ignoring your responsibilities. Ignoring your family."

Taking a deep breath, she finally lost her smile. "Despite how difficult you make it sometimes, Uncle Martin, I do love you. But I'm done being a doormat. And I prefer to spend the holiday with people that will make me feel loved, not abused. Merry Christmas."

She turned around and walked out of the kitchen before he could slam her with more putdowns. Putting on her shoes quickly, she squeaked in surprise when a hand touched her shoulder. Heart pounding, she chuckled a little when she saw it was only Roberta, her aunt's nurse. A true saint for dealing with her uncle every day.

"I wasn't trying to eavesdrop, but I heard the conversation in the kitchen." A gentle, knowing smile touched her lips. "Good for you, Erin. Don't let what he says get to you."

"I would've sunk a long time ago if I did." She hugged Roberta. "I hope you have a great Christmas."

"You, too, dear. He usually leaves on Tuesdays around lunchtime if you want to say goodbye to your aunt then."

"That sounds like a great idea. Thank you, Roberta."

She grabbed one more hug from Roberta, then headed out into the brutal cold once more. She stopped at the grocery store, grabbing a few essentials and some ingredients for a Christmas goodie she had a hankering for. Then she stopped at Betty's craft store and Bernie's hardware store and bought a few more things to complete her errands.

By the time she made it home, the sun was starting to set —and no call from James yet.

But she wasn't going to worry. He said he planned to make her supper and she believed him.

She got to work immediately, making salted nut rolls, a Christmas treat she hadn't had in years. James planned to make the meal. Well, she'd provide the dessert.

After that, she grabbed the other stuff she purchased and started on James' Christmas present. She didn't know if he'd like it, but she had to hope he at least wouldn't hate it.

Hate her.

In the middle of situating some of the things in the pretty Christmas box she purchased, the doorbell rang.

She glanced at her phone sitting on the bed next to her. No missed calls.

Maybe James decided to surprise her by showing up without calling first.

There was an extra giddiness in her step as she made her way to the front door. When she swung it open, she tried not to frown.

Chief Duncan smiled crookedly, an indicator she failed miserably at hiding her disappointment. "Expecting someone else? Sorry."

"Oh, no. Of course not. Come on in, Chief."

Chief Duncan stepped inside, stomping his boots on the

welcome rug, but made no move to go any further in the house. Erin replaced her sadness with a grin.

"Is everything okay?"

He nodded. "You said you wanted to know the outcome when I was done investigating."

"I did."

The grim expression on his face made her heart skip a beat. Her hands started to shake. Wrapping her arms in front of her chest, she refused to lose her smile.

"It wasn't what I expected. I thought I'd tell you in person."

Oh, no.

It couldn't be.

James would never steal drugs.

Yet, by the dismal expression, that's exactly what he was about to say.

MAYBE HE SHOULD'VE CALLED. Showing up unannounced seemed like a very bad idea. What had he been thinking?

He turned around from Erin's front door, shivering, but not from the cold slicing him apart as the wind whipped around.

Regret.

That's what made him tremble.

Before he left town, he would not regret a moment of his time with Erin. He said he'd cook something for her and he meant it. He simply preferred not to cook for her in his dismal rundown house. He had dropped off the Christmas present he bought for her at his house, then drove straight here with the groceries he had purchased to make the perfect chicken wild rice soup. Because right now, with as cold as it was, soup sounded like the best thing to warm them up.

Turning back toward the door, he squared his shoulders and pushed through the anxiety threatening to take over.

He knocked firmly on her door.

This time, he shivered from the sharp sting of wind that whipped around him. But at least it wasn't snowing again. They had enough of that to last them for a month.

The door swung open.

Erin stood there dressed in a cute, silly Christmas sweater. But the frown on her face wasn't too reassuring.

Maybe his first initial reaction was on the mark. He should've never shown up unannounced.

She shook her head as if snapping herself out of some sort of shock, pushed the door open wider, and gestured for him to come inside. "It's freezing out. Come on in."

As soon as he stepped through, he understood her surprise. Chief Duncan stood to the side, although his expression was unreadable.

Damn. His anxiety was so high, he didn't see the chief's car parked outside. His mind had been focused on one thing —Erin. The chief had to have parked on the street because he didn't park in the driveway. He would've noticed an extra vehicle there.

Erin shut the door and took a position by his side, a sweet smile on her face. It was a completely different contrast to her previous look. "Let me hang up your jacket."

Instead of answering, he glanced between her and Chief Duncan. Were they both going to ignore that the chief of police was in her home? Why? What reason would he have to see Erin?

He wanted an answer, but he couldn't seem to find the words to ask.

And he needed his jacket to grab the groceries from his car. He showed up without calling. He didn't want to be presumptuous that she'd want him here by having the groceries in his hand already.

"James?" Erin said softly, hesitantly. "Your jacket?"

He turned his attention away from her and focused solely on Chief Duncan, yet still didn't say a word.

Chief Duncan returned his stare, his expression still undecipherable. Then a smile appeared out of nowhere. "It's good to see you, James. I'm glad you came."

"You are?" Frowning, he couldn't understand why the chief of police would be happy to see him unless he was looking forward to arresting him for something. It wouldn't be the first time he got arrested.

"Chief..." Erin whispered his name so low James' arms flushed with goosebumps. Why did she sound scared?

Chief Duncan kept smiling as if nothing were wrong. Yet Erin's tone of voice said something was seriously wrong. She knew what he was going to say.

"I'm sorry to hear you were fired from the hospital."

James scoffed, rolling his eyes. "Sure you are."

Shifting his stance, still relaxed and unthreatening, Chief Duncan chuckled. "I'm not in the habit of lying. I am sorry. It's never okay when someone is treated the way you were. I did some digging into the matter."

Erin grabbed his hand, squeezing. He didn't look at her, wondering why she needed to hold his hand, offer comfort for some reason. He kept his gaze directly on Chief Duncan, preparing himself for the worst.

"Yeah, Aiden mentioned he asked you to look into it. It's not necessary. It's done and over with."

"It is." Chief Duncan sighed, yet his lips were still curled upward. "I know who stole the drugs. And Dr. Pearson is doing what he should've done in the first place. Report it to the proper channels."

James shrugged like he didn't care. But he did. And he wanted to know who stole the drugs but refused to ask. Maybe it was better if he didn't know.

Chief Duncan nodded as if he understood what his simple shrug meant. "Dr. Pearson's wife took the drugs. She's had a drug problem for a while now, ever since she hurt her back in a car accident over a year ago. She's also having an affair with Dr. Colton, which is why he lied saying he saw you leave the pharmacy after hours."

"Seriously?" Erin said with the shock lacing her tone. "You learned all of that after I left. How?"

"Wait?" James tugged on her hand, waiting for her to look at him. "Left? Why were you at the hospital?"

A tender smile adorned her beautiful face. "It doesn't matter right now. We'll talk about it later. But I was there when Chief Duncan confronted Dr. Pearson."

"Yes, and when that didn't work, I talked to Dr. Colton, who caved pretty quickly with the threat of getting arrested. He lied for her because Dr. Pearson suspected they were having an affair and they thought this would distract him."

"So I lost my job, everyone believing I took these drugs, because two people wanted to keep having sex without getting caught? Is that what you're telling me?" James asked, disgusted. He couldn't wait to get out of this hellhole. People using him as a scapegoat because it was easy.

Chief Duncan looked uncomfortable, wincing. "Basically. Dr. Pearson was afraid of losing a great doctor, believing his story without much evidence. Now he's out a good doctor and an administrator for the hospital. Not to mention, probably getting a divorce." He cleared his throat.

"Not that you care about that. I truly am sorry you were dragged into the mess."

Perhaps Chief Duncan really was. Perhaps he wasn't such a bad guy. Maybe Aiden had the right idea to bring the matter to Chief Duncan. He solved it within a few hours.

It didn't mean he'd admit any of that. But maybe a quick thank you wouldn't hurt.

"Appreciate it." That was about as close to a thank you he could muster. But he was curious about something. "Why did you come here to tell Erin?"

"She asked me to." Chief Duncan took a few steps toward the front door. "And she fought like hell for you in front of Dr. Pearson. Have a good night." Then he left.

Another shiver rippled through him when the door shut, leaving behind a blast of cold air.

"Can I take your jacket now?"

He looked at Erin, bringing her hand to his mouth, pressing a light kiss to it. How did he get so lucky to have found such a wonderful woman?

"Can I bring in the groceries I bought first? I still owe you a meal."

Oh, they had a lot to talk about, but it was something they could do over supper.

A smile lit up her face.

"Yes, I'm starving."

Damn. He was, too.

But not for food.

Just her. His sweet Erin. So fierce and protective. But also kind and thoughtful.

18

ERIN WIPED her mouth with a napkin, then set it down on her lap. "I am so glad there's going to be leftovers of this soup. So delicious. Thank you, James."

The handsome smile on his face filled her aching heart up a little more each time he displayed it as the night went on. It wasn't easy at first. It took a little teasing, tickling him, making funny jokes, dancing in front of him with her silly Christmas sweater as he cooked to get him to even crack a smile.

She couldn't blame him for his morose expression and his low mood after finding out why he was fired. They still hadn't broached the subject yet. She didn't want to bring it up, but she knew they needed to talk about it.

"I'll make it anytime you want." His grin said it was true, but the sadness in his eyes said he couldn't. Not if he was leaving, something he didn't want to talk about.

Well, she didn't want to talk about it yet either. It would ruin her Christmas present for him.

He wiped his mouth with a napkin as he put his spoon down in the bowl. It made a light clattering noise as it fell to the side. "Are you ready to tell me why you went to the hospital?"

Not really was on the tip of her tongue.

But she couldn't ignore it. She couldn't lie to him like other people had.

"I quit. I told you I was."

His jaw clenched and his eyes filled with rage. "Damn it, Erin. You shouldn't have done that. Not for me."

"Maybe it was for me, too. My life isn't perfect either. Whether people want to make it look like their life is perfect, it's not." Her lips thinned into a tight line. "Look at Dr. Pearson. It looked like he had a fairytale life. Great job. Beautiful wife. No worries. Well, that was all completely wrong."

His gaze drew down to the table, sadness filling his entire posture. "What now, Erin? What are you going to do?"

"What I always do. Forge on. That job didn't define me. This town doesn't define me. And it certainly doesn't define you."

He met her gaze. "It seems like it does. Not many people believed in me."

"Only the people that matter believed in you. All those other people...well, they can go step in a pile of dog shit."

Laughter broke out, a huge smile on his face. "You surprise me all the time. Showing up at the cabin. Refusing to let me run away from my problems. Making me laugh when I don't want to."

"Are we ready to move on? Can you not be mad at me for quitting?"

His laughter and smile disappeared. "But where do we move on from here? I can't—"

"How about the bedroom? Or the living room for a cup

of hot chocolate and a movie. It doesn't matter what room we move to."

She knew he wasn't talking about right here and now, but she didn't want to talk about the future. Not yet, anyway. All they would do was keep arguing and she was tapped out emotionally. Dealing with Dr. Pearson, her uncle that always drained her. She was ready to veg out and relax with James' warm arms around her.

"I heard I do make a mean hot chocolate," he said with a sly smile.

"Well, I'm willing to find out if you're willing to make some."

He stood up with the bowl in his hand. "Sounds good. Let me clean up. You go pick out a movie."

"I'll help. You made this delicious meal. It's only fair."

They worked together as a team, bringing the dirty dishes from the dining room to the kitchen. James started making the hot chocolate while she loaded the dishes in the dishwasher. It didn't take too long to get everything cleared away.

After adding extra marshmallows in her cup, they both took their drinks to the living room and took a seat on the couch. Snuggling under the blanket, being careful with their drinks, Erin grabbed the remote from the coffee table.

"There has to be a good Christmas movie on one of these channels. I'm too lazy to dig in my movies."

He nodded, blowing on his hot chocolate. "Surf away." He took a sip of his drink. "Tell me what else you did today."

"What makes you think I did anything else?"

He had one hand on her knee while the other held his cup. His hand on her knee lightly squeezed in comfort. "I'm the master at hiding my emotions. You, not so much."

She chuckled, her head falling back as her laughter got

louder. "You're terrible at hiding your emotions. You're an open book."

"Well, so are you, sweetheart." He kissed the side of her head, chuckling with her.

Sweetheart.

Oh, how she loved the sound of the endearment on his lips.

"I went to the hospital and quit my job. I went shopping for some groceries and Christmas presents. I also went..." Blowing out a breath, her finger paused on the button on the controller.

"Yeah? You went where?" Another tender kiss touched the side of her head.

"I saw my uncle in all his disapproving glory." She would leave it at that. Because if she told him the rest, she'd have to confess she was moving away, too. With him.

"Want me to kick his ass for you? I can."

Chuckling, she met his concerned gaze, knowing he was only teasing to make her smile. "That's so sweet of you to offer. But no. He wasn't so bad when I first moved here. I don't know why he's so cruel with his words. Maybe it's the only way he knows how to deal with his stress. I don't know."

James looked like he wanted to avert his eyes, but he didn't. He held her gaze strong. "Yeah, we all deal with stress differently. I know that firsthand. Alcohol was my best friend for stress."

"And now?"

A crooked smile emerged. "I like video games."

"I rock at racing games."

He tilted his head, playfulness sparkling in his eyes. "I'd school you in a heartbeat, sweetheart."

Erin sat up, her mouth in a wide circle of surprise, the

challenge filling her veins. "Well, I happen to have an old school gaming system in my closet. I'd rather beat you in every racing game I own than watch a movie."

"You like video games?"

"I do." And even if she hadn't, she would've learned to love them for him.

Because she loved him.

But it wasn't necessary because she used to play video games all the time with her sister growing up. She loved all kinds of games. The more time she spent with James, getting to know him, the more she realized how much they had in common. How right the decision she was making to move with him was.

His hand on her knee trailed slowly up her leg. "I thought you were perfect before. Now you are beyond perfection."

Oh, this man with his sweet, tender words.

"Show me where it's at. I'll get it set up."

Smiling, she set her cup on the coffee table and headed for her bedroom. She had to dig for the box that held her gaming system, which was tucked away in the back corner.

It didn't take James long to set it up, and they were racing shortly after. Teasing each other mercifully, they played well into the night. She held her own, her skills a bit rusty from not playing as regularly as he did.

When James saw the clock on the wall, his happiness faltered. "It's a lot later than I thought. I should probably—"

"Spend the night." Grabbing one of his hands that clutched the console in a death grip, she smiled. "You should definitely spend the night. I've gotten used to sleeping next to you."

"It was only two days," he said with a grin, leaning closer to kiss her. "But I got used to sleeping next to you, too."

"So that's settled."

"Are you sure?"

Grabbing the front of his shirt with both hands, she pulled him closer, laughing. "I'm always sure when it comes to you."

Pressing her lips against his, she told him how much she wanted him to spend the night. James took control of the kiss as he wrapped his arms around her. She had to scoot closer, entangling her legs around his waist for a more comfortable position. James deepened the kiss, making her body ache for more. Much more.

"Let's go to bed," she whispered against his lips.

He answered her with a kiss, then stood up with her securely in his arms. "This will be the first time we actually sleep in a bed together."

She giggled. "I didn't mind the floor, but a real bed will be nice. Let me turn off the TV."

He bent a little, letting her grab the controller from the coffee table, and with a quick press of the button, the TV went dark. Then he ventured down the hallway and to her bedroom.

Gently laying her down on the bed, he kissed her. "I could get used to this every night."

A smile splayed across her lips. Oh, she could, too. She planned to get used to it every single night. He just didn't know it yet.

"You're still spending Christmas Day with me, right?"

Brushing her hands down his back, relishing in the fact that she could make this handsome, devilish man shiver with delight, she nodded. "Of course. How about tomorrow as well, for Christmas Eve? A lazy day playing video games."

"A woman after my own heart. I am the stupidest man alive for waiting so long to make a move on you."

She slapped him playfully on the ass. "Hey, buster. I made the first move. I followed you to the cabin in the middle of a snowstorm."

Grinning a sexy grin, his eyes sparkling with delight, he chuckled. "And I'm so glad you did."

His lips met hers.

A sweet, slow kiss that melted her heart and told her he cared.

She knew he cared about her.

But how much?

Would he want her to come with him?

Christmas couldn't come fast enough. She was dying to give him his present.

19

"WHAT CAN I DO TO HELP?"

His sister waved a hand at him with a silly smile. "Nothing. I have the turkey in the oven and everything else is almost done. I want you to relax. Go hang out with Erin. I have this covered."

But that was the problem. Hanging out by Erin. He was dying to give her his present and nervous all at the same time. For some crazy reason, they decided to give each other their presents at his sister's house rather than before they left her house. Well, it had been his idea. He thought she might be more agreeable once she opened her present if she was around other people. Hopefully, anyway.

Besides grabbing a bag of clothes and toiletry items, he hadn't been to his house since leaving the cabin. He wanted to keep living with her. Anywhere. Even in this dumb town if she wanted to stay.

That's how much he loved Erin. Spending the entire day Christmas Eve with her yesterday, he knew without a doubt he couldn't live without her. So when he went home to grab more clothes, he grabbed her Christmas present as well. He was dying to give it to her. In the next breath, he was absolutely terrified.

"Out, James. I don't need help."

Listening to his sister, he left the kitchen and took a seat next to Erin on the couch. Aiden excused himself, almost as if he knew James wanted time alone with her.

He did. Kind of.

"What's wrong?" She grabbed one of his hands, linking fingers with him.

"I wanted to help my sister and she wouldn't let me."

Sweet laughter filled the room. "That's why it looks like you're sad?"

He frowned. "I'm not sad."

"You're frowning."

Well, damn, he was, but he wasn't sad. Nervous was more like it.

"Are you having fun?"

Tilting her head with a sincere smile, she nodded. "I always have fun with you. It's been a great day so far." She grasped his hand with a firm grip as she pressed her lips together in a motherly disapproving manner. "But it's not a great day when you're sad."

Chuckling, he lifted their hands and pressed a kiss to the back of her hand. "I'm not sad." Nervous. Very, very nervous. Of course, he couldn't say that.

Turning his attention to the tree where his present sat for her, he gave himself a mental pep talk, urging himself on. Then he looked at her. "Let's open our presents."

Looking at him with an odd frown, then at the tree, she said, "Shouldn't we wait for Theresa and Aiden? I mean, isn't that why you wanted to open them here?"

Yes and no. But he didn't want to wait anymore. Now he wasn't sure if having an audience, especially one being his sister, was the best idea. His nerves were jangling like a holly jolly song going nuts. He had to get it over with.

"I want to open them now. Theresa and Aiden aren't going to mind."

A tremble touched his hand. Oh, good to know. She was just as nervous as him.

Her eyes were still trained on the tree. "Well, okay. If you're sure." Then she whipped her beautiful emerald green eyes his way. "Because if you're not, we can wait. Because it's okay to wait. You know. Because I don't mind waiting. But if you want to do it, that's cool. Because I'm cool with whatever."

He let go of her hand and cupped her cheeks, pulling her closer. Landing a soft kiss to her lips, a low, barely audible sigh escaped. "You are so damn adorable when you get like this."

Biting her lip, she giggled. "Like what? Because I'm totally not like anything right now. I'm totally normal. I have no idea what you're talking about. I'm totally cool."

Kissing her again, a little harder, a little more insistent, he savored how wonderful she felt in his arms. Something he always wanted until the day he died.

Letting her go reluctantly, he lowered his hands from her face and then stood up, grabbed the presents from under the tree, and sat back down by her.

"You were saying *because* a lot. Then *totally* became your new favorite word. It's adorable. I love it," he said huskily, handing her the present he wrapped kind of lamely. But hey, he didn't do presents often, and usually only with Theresa and Aiden. And it didn't matter how it looked wrapped, it was what was inside that mattered. So she'd have to deal with the crooked folding of the paper and the excess use of tape that he plastered everywhere.

She bit her lip again as she looked down at the present. "I talk too much when I get nervous. Terrible trait."

He touched her chin, holding it until she looked at him. "Totally adorable."

A sweet smile lit up her face like the bright white lights on Theresa and Aiden's Christmas tree. "Open mine first. Please."

Shaking his head, he let go of her chin and tapped the present in her hands. "You go first. I insist. You're not the only one nervous, Erin."

Delicate laughter filled the room. "You're nervous, too? We're both so silly. It's a present."

"Right. It is. So we both have nothing to worry about. Go on. Open mine up." He gestured again at the present, hoping she couldn't hear the pounding of his heart beating so loudly he swore it was going to pop right out of his chest.

She took her time taking off the wrapping paper, a little tremble in her hands here and there as she did. When she finally got it all off, she tossed it to the floor and opened the plain white box he had found tucked in the back of his closet. One of those boxes his sister had used one time, giving him a shirt or something. He was glad he saved it. It would've been even harder to wrap the present without a box.

Looking at the gift inside with a puzzled look, she traced the top of the black-edged frame with her finger.

"It's for your diploma."

Jerking her gaze at him, she shook her head, still confused. "I don't even know where my high school diploma is."

"Not that one." He smiled, hoping he didn't give her the dumbest present ever. "For college."

"I didn't finish college."

"Well, you still can."

"James..." She touched the edge of the frame again, anticipation twinkling in her eyes. "I don't even know what I want to do anymore."

"You'll figure it out. Anything you pick, you'll do wonderful at. I just know it." He shrugged, keeping his laughter light and carefree. God, what a dumb present now that he thought about it. "And you quit your job. You're free to move."

With me. He couldn't say that yet. He still had to convince her going back to college was the right thing to do. Otherwise, she didn't have a good enough reason to come with him. This had been the only reason he could come up with, albeit a very dumb one.

Her eyes tilted up, catching his anxious gaze. "I am free to move." Her gaze darted to the gift in his lap. "Open your gift."

"So, you'll go back to college?"

"It's a big decision. I have to think about it." She touched his hand and moved it toward the gift. "Open your gift now. I insist."

Nodding, he opened his gift much faster than she had, wanting to get it over with. He wanted to talk more about college and persuading her to leave. Because once she agreed, he'd say that's where he happened to be moving, too. It was the perfect plan. Sort of.

Taken aback by the contents once he lifted the lid, he frowned, confused. Pulling out a road map first, he started laughing when he saw what looked like a small scrapbook and some stickers.

"Umm..." He had no idea what to say. He wasn't a crafty kind of guy.

"Silly, right?" Erin laughed, too. "It made sense in my head when I was buying it."

"I've never scrapbooked in my life." He picked up the stickers. "Stickers are cool, though."

One sheet held different road signs with sayings like *We Made It*, *Cool Destination*, *On to the Next Stop*, and so on. One sheet was filled with loving home sayings like *Home Sweet Home* and *Home is Where the Heart Is*. There were two more sheets of stickers with other cheesy sayings. He started laughing again.

"You want me to scrapbook my trip after I leave?"

She touched her frame with a delicate finger. "Apparently you want me to go back to college."

They both gave each other odd presents, yet perfect for each other. Because if you put them together, they fit just right.

"I want you to go to college so I can pick that as the place where I move." There. He said it. He put his heart on the line. "Because I don't want to lose you, but I have to leave. Yet, I want to be wherever you are, Erin. I love you."

Her bottom lip started wobbling as if she were going to cry. Shit. He didn't want to see her cry. She sniffed, then wiped at her eyes. "I love you, too."

Whoa. Seriously? He didn't expect to hear it back right away. He thought he had his work cut out for him.

"Really?"

"Of course," she said, laughing, wiping at her eyes again. Then she pointed at the map. "I thought we could close our eyes and put our finger down, and wherever it landed, that's where we would move. And yes, scrapbook our journey."

"Our...journey?" He looked down at the map and other

things she had put inside the box. A box filled with road trip adventure supplies.

"Oh, I totally planned to move with you how many days ago. Why do you think I quit my job? You're stuck with me, mister, whether you like it or not."

Glancing up, he grinned, reaching for her. Wrapping a warm hand around her neck, he pulled her closer, landing a soft kiss to her lips. "I wouldn't want to be stuck with anyone but you. So we'll close our eyes and pick a spot on the map. It better have a college because you're going back."

"But if it doesn't—"

"We'll close our eyes and try again." He leaned his forehead against hers, rubbing her neck, aching to do so much more. "You didn't say it, but I heard it anyway. You regret not finishing college. We should never regret anything."

"As long as we're together."

He kissed her. Slowly and with all the love he had for her. "I love you, Erin. I don't deserve you, but I'm selfish. It's a terrible trait of mine that I can't fix. I'm so selfish, I don't want to leave without you."

"We both have terrible traits, then."

"No, yours is adorable."

Laughing, she shook her head, then snatched another kiss. "This turned out to be one of the best Christmases ever."

"Yeah, it did."

The best thing that ever happened was getting fired, as crazy as it sounded. Because then he never would've escaped to a cabin out in the middle of nowhere. Erin would've never followed him to check on him. They would've never been stuck while a blizzard stormed its way through town. They would've never found each other and how much they loved each other.

"Merry Christmas, Erin. I'm looking forward to our new adventure."

A bright, sweet smile filled her beautiful face. "Me, too. I might even help you scrapbook. I won't make you do it all."

He laughed, loving the feeling of being so happy, something he hadn't felt in the longest time.

Scrapbooking? Ha! He couldn't see himself lifting a finger to do anything of the sort.

Then Erin smiled and laughed with him.

And the idea didn't seem so preposterous.

As silly as the gift was he had given her, and vice versa, he got one gift he would never trade for the world.

Her heart and her love.

Merry Christmas to him.

EPILOGUE

Erin blew out a breath, her lips making a rumbling sound as she did. A warm hand slid into hers, squeezing.

"You can do this. It's important that you do. Trust me. It wasn't easy asking Theresa for forgiveness for the things I did to her, but I did. I had to own up to how I treated her. I felt better afterward."

Looking at James sitting in the driver's seat, the concern and worry in his eyes, she knew she could do this when he shared a part of himself with her. He didn't always like to talk about his past, but when he did, she loved him a little bit more each time. She felt like she was going to burst open one of these times with how much she loved him.

"Maybe she doesn't even care about me anymore. Like, for real. She doesn't care."

She wouldn't be surprised if her sister slammed the door in her face. She said some terrible things the day she left five years ago. Of course, her sister said some nasty things in return. It had been a blowout of all blowouts they ever had as sisters. They were both so hardheaded, she figured they had both been waiting for the other to make the first move.

"Her loss if she doesn't."

She blew out another trembling breath, then nodded. "Okay. I'm ready. For real."

He looked out the window. Snow was lightly falling, which had started about twenty minutes ago. The forecast didn't say it was supposed to turn terrible or make the roads too dangerous, but she knew they shouldn't take any chances. She had to get this over with, hopefully with her sister's forgiveness, and then hit the road to their new home.

They were leaving.

Scratch that. They already left. This was just a pit stop on the way to their destination. James already made the hard goodbyes to his family. She said goodbye to her aunt and sat with her for a good hour before she had to leave because she hadn't wanted to run into her uncle. She had already said her goodbye to him.

"I can go with you."

"I'd love that. For real." Another heavy breath released. "But I should do it by myself."

He smiled, kissed her hand, then winked. "You got this. She loves you. How couldn't she? You're so damn lovable."

"Stop with the mushiness," she said with a laugh as she let go of his hand and put on her mittens. "Okay. I'm going. For real this time."

Before she could change her mind, she opened the car door and stepped out into the blistering cold as the snow pelted her face. She shut the door on James' laughter. Oh, she knew why he was laughing. She couldn't stop saying *for real*. Just another indicator of how nervous she was, repeating such silly words. *For real?* Geez. Could she get any more ridiculous?

With brisk steps, she walked to the front door and knocked—loudly—just so she didn't have to do it again because she didn't know if she'd have the strength.

A few seconds later, the door swung open.

Her sister's jaw dropped.

"Hey, Aria. It's me," she said somewhat awkwardly as a low chuckle came out with her dumb words. *It's me.* Really? All those speeches she prepared and that's all she could say.

She just got more ridiculous.

Then without warning, her sister pulled her into a hug. "I'm so glad it's you. I missed you."

The cold wind biting into her backside didn't even penetrate as she wrapped her arms around her sister, soaking up her warmth, and dare she hope, her forgiveness without even saying the words yet.

Aria backed away, her hands still on her arms, and then looked over her shoulder. "Who's that in the car? Tell him to come inside. You're not leaving yet."

"Okay. Sure."

She had to get over this speechlessness. Aria waved to James. Erin turned, waving for him to come as well. He didn't ignore either of them, exiting the car and taking a spot next to her on the porch steps.

"Come on in."

They followed Aria inside. Erin was glad to be in from the cold.

"Well, aren't you going to introduce me to this handsome fellow?"

Erin smiled as she looped her arm through James' arm. Aria had always been the flirty one between the two of them. Erin was always telling her this boy liked her and that boy liked her when all she saw was a good friend. She had always been the focused one, too. Her eye on the prize, no matter what she wanted. Boys. A job. Good grades. So darn focused. And Erin, the unorganized, flighty one. Tomboy, friends with all the boys, never seeing them as potential boyfriends. Quick to decisions with no thought process to it. They were so completely different. Yet, she loved her sister.

"This is James. My boyfriend."

Aria's eyes lit up with happiness, a sight she had sorely missed seeing.

"So lovely to meet you, James," Aria said, holding out her hand.

James shook it. "You, too. Erin talks about you all the time."

Sort of a lie, but she wasn't about to contradict him. She talked about Aria on occasion because talking about her always made her feel guilty about how she acted all those years ago.

But his words made her sister smile even more, making her look more beautiful than two seconds ago. Her sister *was* beautiful. Always had been. Even with no makeup on, unlike her. She always looked like a ragged doll if she didn't at least put on a bit of mascara and eye shadow.

Despite always looking beautiful, always flirting in a nice, unthreatening way, she never felt jealous or worried that Aria would try to steal her boyfriends. Because her sister loved her too much to do something so callous and mean.

How did it go so wrong? How did they lose so many years together? No talking or laughing or acting like sisters?

"I'm so sorry, Aria." Her voice cracked as her eyes filled with water. "I'm so sorry about the things I said. I'm so sorry I stayed away for so long. I'm so sorry that—"

"Stop, Erin." Aria grabbed her arm, her grip firm and unyielding, her eyes filling with tears as well. "You're repeating yourself." She giggled. "You don't have to keep saying *so sorry* to me. I'm sorry, too. We both said things we shouldn't have and you're here now. Let's move on. Let's have a drink and tell each other what's been going on for the last five years."

All her worries and fears rushed out in one large breath as her sister's words calmed her down. She should've known Aria would make this easy. She always had with anything put in front of her. Erin felt like she should hate her sister for being the perfect sister in the family, but she didn't. She envied her a bit, though.

"That sounds like a great plan. A nice cup of coffee would be awesome." As much as she'd love to have a small glass of wine with her sister and reminisce, she didn't drink when she was around James.

Looking at James, she tugged on his arm, smiling. "It's starting to snow. Maybe you can try to find a hotel on your phone."

They hadn't intended to stay the night, but she didn't want to leave yet. She wanted to catch up with her sister. Laugh, cry, indulge in sweet treats while they talked the night away.

"Oh, stop, Erin. You can stay here." Aria squeezed her arm, then let go, wiping at her eyes. "I insist. I saw a moving trailer attached to your vehicle. Are you moving back?"

This part would be harder than she imagined.

"No, we're moving..." She laughed, still surprised where James' finger had landed and how happy they both had been when they opened their eyes. "We're moving to Florida. For a change. For a new adventure."

"For Erin to finish college."

Giving him a side glare, she chuckled when he widened his eyes as if she would be doing that whether she wanted to or not. Currently, she would not be going back to school. She planned to in the fall, but right now she wanted to find a nice place to rent, get a decent job, and figure out what she wanted to major in. Becoming a nurse was in the past. She didn't want to do that anymore.

"Well, it is starting to snow and we might get more tomorrow. I'd hate for you to get stuck here a few days when you didn't intend to. Let me pack a bag." Aria turned around.

"Wait? What?"

Aria looked over her shoulder. "Road trip time. We can talk all we want in the car."

Erin let go of James' arm and propped a hand to her hip. "Since when does my sister do random, unsuspected things? I'm the flighty one. You're the planner."

"You, my beautiful sister, just showed up after five years of not speaking, seeing, or even hearing about what was going on in your life. I'm entitled to some spontaneity if I want." A huge, bright smile spread across her face. "And right now I want to go on a road trip." Aria frowned. "Unless you don't want me coming with."

Erin squealed in delight. "Are you kidding? This will be so much fun." Then she calmed down and looked at James. "As long as you're okay with it."

"Of course."

The sweet sparkle in his eyes said he wasn't lying, that he was happy to see her sister forgiving her and wanting to come with.

Erin hugged him. "Thank you."

He kissed the top of her head. "Always. I love you."

"I love you, too." Then she looked at her sister. "Let me help you pack."

Following her sister to her room, she couldn't wait to

start this new adventure with a man that supported her in every single way.

———

DON'T MISS THE NEXT BOOK IN THIS HEARTWARMING HOLIDAY SERIES!
SNOWFLAKES AND SHOTS

FOR ELLIOT & LYNN'S STORY
MERRY ME
A HOLIDAY ROMANCE NOVEL, #1

He never knew a simple gift left on his porch step would mend his wounded heart.

Hiding his dislike for the holidays isn't easy, especially when Chief Elliot Duncan meets a woman who captures his attention with one sweet smile. Lynn Carpenter is beautiful, strong-willed, and hardworking, and he doesn't know how to return her gift that was left on his porch by mistake. As Christmas approaches, it doesn't take much for the holiday spirit to seep in, not when Lynn makes it so effortless with her excitement. The only thing he wants for Christmas this year is her heart. But between his meddling father and the need to take care of her, something she passionately resists, he knows it won't be that simple. He's up for the challenge, because losing Lynn is unacceptable.

FOR AIDEN & THERESA'S STORY
MISTLETOE MAGIC
A HOLIDAY ROMANCE NOVEL, #2

A mistletoe. A kiss. This just might be the start of a beautiful Christmas.

Theresa might not make the best pot of coffee in town, but people still flock to the diner for a cup, even Officer Crowl, who rarely displays a smile since his fiancé died. She'll never be able to win his heart, but it's hard to resist him, especially when he kisses her under the mistletoe. Well, on the cheek, but that has to count for something...right?

Staying busy keeps Officer Aiden Crowl sane. Because when he's idle or alone, he thinks, and nothing good comes from that. Everyone thinks he's the perfect man. They think he's broken because she's gone. He is, just not for the reason they believe. Every time he walks into the diner, one sweet smile from Theresa erases some of the pain. He should stay away from her. Far away. But what is he supposed to do when they're standing under a mistletoe? Kiss her, of course.

FOR BENTLEY & EMMA'S STORY
CHRISTMAS WISH
A HOLIDAY ROMANCE NOVEL, #3

*What if you had one wish granted for Christmas? What would
it be?*

Acting reckless isn't something Bentley Wilson is known for,
but when he runs back into a burning building to save a
little girl's puppy after specifically told not to do so, that's
exactly how most of the town sees him, especially the fire
chief who insists he has to help with the annual Christmas
party because of his behavior. Throw in the fact the woman
he's pined over for too long is getting married, this holiday is
going to go down as one of the worst. Until he meets Emma
Brookes. She's feisty, headstrong, and holds so much pain
hidden in the depths of her beautiful green eyes. He wants
nothing more than to erase her sadness. But it's already a
season of disaster, and every time they're together, they spar
like two warriors dueling to the death. Despite that, he likes
the challenge, the crazy way she makes him feel. Before the
holiday is over, he vows to get his one Christmas wish. That
she never leaves his side.

One last shot at love...

Stu doesn't have many regrets in life—not even the fact he never decorates his bar for the holidays. But when a bar fight turns into needing medical attention, he's put face-to-face with the one woman he's tried to avoid for the last fifteen years. Okay, so maybe he regrets a few things. He should've never walked away from her. It only took a good knock to his head to make him see clearly. He's going to win Chasity's heart once again. It doesn't matter that she's not going to make it easy; he's up for the challenge. Bring on the bets and all the Christmas spirit he can handle. Except, one person doesn't like the idea of them together—the same person that had him walking away from her all those years ago.

FOR MASE & HOPE'S STORY
HOLIDAY HOPE
A HOLIDAY ROMANCE NOVEL, #6

Let the merriment begin...Operation Holiday Hope commence.

Life hasn't been the same since she quit her job working for the tyrant mayor, but Hope Bronson is trying her best. She's attempting to embrace the holiday spirit and pretend she's happy when, in reality, she feels stuck in a rut. And why? She can't even explain it to herself, let alone to anyone else, without risking being called a drama queen. And men... don't even get her started. Talk about bad choices every. Single. Time. Except...maybe one guy, but she can't trust her own judgment. It doesn't matter that everyone tells her he's a good one. She's leery of opening herself up to another bad decision—unless he can convince her otherwise.

Mase Brandt can't believe his luck when he's asked to fix a Nativity scene for the church. The one and only woman to steal his heart with ease works there. A few months ago, she shut him out with little fanfare. This time, he's not giving up so easily. The holidays are a joyous time of year. He'll use anything and everything to his advantage to win her heart. He knows she won't make a moment of it easy on him. But that's okay. He has a few tricks up his sleeve. Let the festivities begin.

There's no such thing as too much holiday cheer...right?

If there's one thing Cam is good at, it's working with his hands. So making a sleigh for the woman who loves Christmas with a passion seems like a foolproof plan to win her heart. He's done being stuck in the friend zone. Except he's a little rusty with dating. After keeping women at a distance for so long, he's going to need more help than he realized. Who knew he'd get it from where he least expected it—her twin boys. This should be easy-peasy. But one thing Cam has learned: nothing ever works out like he plans.

Serenity doesn't like it known, but she hates Christmas. With a passion. The last thing she can do is let anyone know, especially her boys. She'd never ruin the holiday for them. Besides faking holiday cheer, she finds herself having to resist the one man who is impossible to resist. Cam is everything she always wanted in a guy: kind, caring, always there for her when she needs him. But they're friends, and losing him from her life can't happen. Venturing into the sex-zone would ruin it all. If there is one thing she's good at, it's pretending. All she has to do is make him believe being friends is for the best.

ABOUT THE AUTHOR

I'm a *USA Today* Bestselling Author that loves to write contemporary romance and romantic suspense novels, although I am partial to romantic suspense. I even dabble in paranormal. Honestly, I love anything that has to do with romance. As long as there's a happy ending, I'm a happy camper. And insta-love...yes, please! I love baseball (Go Twins!) and creating awesome crafts. I graduated with a Bachelor's Degree in Criminal Justice, working in that field for several years before I became a stay-at-home mom. I have a few more amazing stories in the works. If you would like to learn more about me and my books, head to my website by scanning the QR code. Thanks for reading!

Scan me